Stranger on the Island

Book Two of the Island Series

Jonathan Ross

Also by Jonathan Ross

Death in a Carolina Swamp

The Jumbee's Daughter

Scent of Death

New Girl on the Island (Book One of the Island Series)

For more information about Jonathan Ross and his novels, please visit www.jonathanrossnovels.com

Published by High Ground Initiatives, Arnold, MD USA

With love, to Marna

Acknowledgments
To Donna, for her kind editorial assistance.

Invitation

Hi,

I invite you to receive one of my tropical-island short stories and a free subscription to my monthly newsletter. The newsletter gives you news on my upcoming books, reduced purchase price during book launches, glimpses behind-the-scenes, and suggestions of other books you may like. Of course, you may unsubscribe at any time. To accept, simply go to this URL:
https://www.subscribepage.com/jonathanross-newgirl

Jonathan Ross

CHAPTER 1

Amid sounds of chirping insects, fluttering parakeets, and the whisper of breeze through leafy canopy, Sophie heard a sharp crack.

That's strange, she thought, at first only curious. An animal? She'd come across stray dogs in the jungle-like growth on her walks before. Some were friendly, some not. But the rainforest critters had stopped their singing. They sensed an intruder. A stealthy one, furtive. Probably not a dog.

She breathed silently. Ignored the sweat filming her upper lip. Swiveled left and right. Searched. Listened.

Too quiet.

Then another sharp crack. *It's a person. Messing with my mind.* Reflexively, she raised her hands to chest level, lightly fisted, ready to defend herself.

Insects started up again. Two bright-green parrots zoomed overhead. She searched the surrounding tangle of trees and vines, the broad curving leaves. Looking for anything straight or regular. Any color other than green. Any movement.

Nothing seemed out of place. And yet...

Damn. I should have invited Richard along. No, he was off island on a charter. Besides, she had been in this valley before. It had seemed peaceful those times – birds, foliage, and lizards, all in beautiful harmony.

But today was different, something inexplicable caused a nauseous flutter in her belly. She strained to hear more sounds of a stealthy approach. Too bad she hadn't borrowed one of Richard's pistols.

She gritted her teeth, frustrated. This was St. Mark for goodness sakes, the tiniest of the US Virgin Islands. End of the line. Where you go for peace. This wasn't downtown Miami. You don't need to carry here for protection. You could walk alone anywhere on the island and know that no one would bother you.

Or was that wishful thinking? Things change. They sure did in St. Thomas, or so she'd been told. It had been another sleepy island in the 1950's. Now their police were constantly on the lookout for drug smugglers.

Her skin crawled as she pondered her options. She considered calling out, hoping to find it was only a lost hiker, maybe even George, up there to cut tree limbs for boat building. No, he would make noise, identify himself and not steal through the woods snapping branches.

"Is anyone there? Hello?" she called out.

No response. Another crack. Closer this time.

Her legs twitched. Adrenalin coursed through her. Fight or flight.

She heard a cough and stepped back and away from the sound. Better to leave than confront. She half-turned to retrace her path, and leave the rainforest, still keeping an eye on the surrounding foliage.

A lizard on a nearby tree cocked its head, peered at her with one glistening eye. It performed a couple of lizard pushups then scampered up and out of sight.

All is normal, she told herself. The woods were safe, a place of peace, a place to lose your cares. *Breathe, Sophie.*

Then she saw a palm frond shift as if someone had moved it aside to get a better view of her. She felt a warning itch between her shoulder blades. God! He's watching me. Why in hell couldn't she see him...it?

A voice inside her screamed, *Get out Sophie! Run!*

She took a quick step, and another, toward town and people – safety. But other footfalls accompanied hers. She broke into a jog and dared to glance back over her shoulder.

A man stood at the edge of vines and tropical leaves, his thin lips curved in a sneer. She tripped to a halt and faced him. Black eyes devoured her, reminding her of a beast, a predator impatient for its next meal. He lunged forward with measured, animal grace but then stopped when she didn't keep on running. She saw the bone handle of a knife poking out of a scabbard at his belt.

"Y'all are trespassing," he growled. *A Southern accent*, she thought vaguely.

"S-sorry. I didn't...but this isn't — "

"Go!" he shouted and took another step toward her, emerging from shadow and into a shaft of sunlight. His two-day stubble and baggy jungle fatigues made him look as though he'd surfaced from deep within a Louisiana bayou.

"Sir, this is Coxon land," she said, feeling violated by his brazen stare. "You're the one who's trespassing."

He charged – no warning. Now she had no choice. Not flight...fight.

Sophie drew a quick breath. Waited until he was nearly even with her, then she pivoted out of his path and guided him past with raised forearms. She breathed relief, but joy quickly turned to claustrophobia as his bulk forced her sideways.

Muttering a curse, he turned and charged again. This time with knife drawn, his arm high, poised to stab.

Sophie counter-charged, glimpsed surprise in his eyes. She leaped up to grasp his raised knife hand with both of hers, digging in with fingernails. Before he could shake her off, she dove under his armpit and twisted at his side. The knife point was now angled upward into the base of his ribs.

He twitched and turned, ruined her position, but put himself off balance. The stench of his sweat fouled her nose. Before he could regain his footing, Sophie made her move. She released his hand, dug her feet into the soft earth, and darted back along the path leading out of the valley. She pumped her legs, eyes forward even as she heard staccato pummeling of jungle boots dogging her.

Sophie redoubled her efforts as the path lifted toward the valley wall. She felt her second wind kick in.

When she reached the valley wall, she paused, her breath ragged. She stopped gulping air for a moment and listened. No pounding feet. No voice.

She jogged up the steep path and left the valley, entering dry woods on a familiar mountain. She continued west on a deer track, and after ten minutes, she left the path and knelt behind a thick clump of underbrush. Listened. Birds chirped, cicadas hummed.

No footfalls, no furtive crunching or cracking. What the hell had that been about? Trespassing? And who was that creature?

She continued quickly along the deer track, toward St. Mark's tiny town. The Coxon home, where she was a guest, lay up the mountain to her right. To the left, at the base of the mountain, lay the Caribbean.

She still felt jittery from her experience and looked forward to being back in town. Small as it was – only five buildings and George's boatyard — people were there. People she knew, who she liked, and who liked her.

Sophie exited the shade of the woods, followed the island's only paved road downhill to the town, and entered a modest white building at its edge. Nailed above the door was a sign: 'John's Dry Goods.' She inhaled welcome scents of packing material, boxes, and kerosene, mixed with musty odors from the building's wooden structure. She took in the plain décor of merchandise aisles and bare walls. Well, it was owned and run by Uncle John, a man. Go figure.

She walked down an aisle to the rear of the store. Leaned her hands against the back counter and stretched her calves, a runner's ritual. God, she wished Uncle John were there, a shoulder to lean on, to shed tears of fear and anger, maybe shame, whatever. She prayed his tests were turning out okay at the hospital on St. Thomas. Was pleased he trusted her with running the store in his absence.

Morning sea air wafted through open jalousie windows. She cruised the aisles, checked for gaps where customers had purchased food. Then nipped into the back room. A third of the modest space was taken up by Uncle John's bed and his armoire, another third by stacked boxes of food and goods for the store, and the rest was available for a person to walk. Sophie retrieved cans of meat and two boxes of cereal and placed them on the shelves.

What bothered her, she decided as she awaited her first customer of the morning, was why the man had attacked her. If he wanted privacy, why not tell her and let her leave? Any idiot must know that pushing her around, much less trying to stab her to death, would bring the police—or in her case, an ex-Marine. She glanced out the front door toward the clearing on the other side of the road, where two dogs and a cackling chicken lazed, her question unanswered.

Island women arrived in ones and twos with their shopping lists and news of families and little adventures and mishaps. Sophie got on with her day.

CHAPTER 2

He deflated his Zodiac boat and concealed the compact result with palm fronds. He rose, wiped sweat from his face. Behind him, the Atlantic foamed over submerged coral heads and splashed onto the narrow beach. Around him lay desiccated bushes and stunted trees, not so unlike the arid desolation of Afghanistan. The only green came from a scattering of coconut palms, their fruit out of reach by all but rats. He gulped sun-warmed water from his Army-surplus canteen. Walked over to the Zodiac's outboard motor and flexed his shoulders.

A vision of the girl appeared in his mind's eye. Blond and beautiful and scared. But she was a scrapper, give her that. Knew a couple moves. Too bad he knew dozens of better ones.

She'd have to die. She'd seen his Afghan *peshkabz* knife, up close and personal. That was his fault in a way, but hell, he'd grown attached to the weapon, depended upon its razor edge and sharp point. Besides, it had a history.

He returned his thoughts to the girl. Her eyes told of intelligence. She would put two and two together and, being a woman, tell her friends about the knife, because it looked exotic to the Western eye. Word would spread and Richard Drake would hear. That was not acceptable. It would ruin the surprise. He shrugged. Two more casualties to cut the chain. It had to be done.

Then freedom to live his life, where and how he wanted. He stooped and hefted the motor, a hundred and sixty-five pounds. No great shakes – he could bench press more than that on a bad day. He stepped over to a black drop cloth, lowered the motor, and wrapped it up. Branches laid on top and around concealed it. Just another pile of rotting vegetation in this hell-hole island. Perfect.

'Perfect.' There was a word. It meant 'nothing wrong.' Just like his plan. Acquire, consolidate, and enjoy. Kill, put up with shitty living conditions. Bumps in the road, to be accepted.

He picked up the last of his mission-essential gear. Night vision goggles, mess kit, tent. Trudged through the undergrowth, avoided deer tracks, gear in left hand, right hand pushed aside branches. Carefully returned each branch to its place, leaving no sign of his passing, and began his trek to the valley.

He reached the rim of the valley, a nearly vertical drop, unreachable by foot except for a couple of switchback paths. He peered down, through gaps in the canopy, and glimpsed trees, vines, and the rainforest floor.

He estimated the length of the valley at around a mile and the width under a half mile. Spurs from the surrounding mountains poked into the valley along its length, making the border of the valley floor undulate in curves.

He traced the progress of a creek that meandered through the center of the valley, north to south, collecting water from multiple brooks, building in size and speed, and emptying out of the south end through a gorge.

The rainforest had its own vegetation and climate, which would no doubt be of interest to certain people, though not to him. All he needed to know was how to navigate the place effectively, meaning the ability to remain invisible from intruders. He snickered at that last thought, recalling the ace he had up his sleeve when it came to invisibility.

He took to the path, feeling exposed but with no other choice.

CHAPTER 3

Sophie's workday meandered to a close late in the afternoon. She'd served the ladies, traded gossip, and counted the till. And now, with her mind empty of duty, she was impatient to see Richard.

She left the store and pulled the door closed. Didn't lock it. No need to on St. Mark.

Maybe not, a voice in her head whispered. The heebie-jeebies from that morning would not go.

The walk to the town dock at the base of the harbor took all of five minutes, which included a brief conversation with a friend and patting the dogs that lounged under the tree across from the store.

She perched on the worn concrete, dangled her legs, and felt cool droplets from gentle waves lapping the structure. To her right stood three ancient stone buildings and past those, George's boatyard, its hammers and saws now quiet for the day.

Sophie kicked herself for venturing into the rainforest alone. Wondered where she'd heard of it anyway. Oh yeah, George mentioned it as a must-see. She should have asked him to show her.

She sighed, gazed through the harbor at the glistening Caribbean. Finally, she spotted the single mast and white hull of Richard's sailboat, CAPRICE. She stood and waved. He entered the harbor and tied up to his mooring buoy, and clambered into his dingy.

A minute later, he climbed onto the dock, smiled that special way, and took her into his arms. He smelled of salt, sweat, and his own scent. God, she loved him. After his third kiss, he pulled back, and held her shoulders. His eyes clouded with concern.

"Something's wrong, Sophie. What is it? Are you okay? My God. What's this bruise on your arm?"

"I've had a terrible experience."

His voice came out ragged. "You're scaring me, Sophie."

"Can we go someplace?"

"The Pirate's Rest?"

"Sure."

He wrapped a comforting arm around her as they walked into the pub and sat at a table out back, on the waterside deck.

"You want a beer?" he asked as they sat.

"Yes, at least a beer."

A minute later, Daniel, who owned the pub with his wife, placed two beers in front of each of them and murmured, "Looks like that kind of day." He departed quietly.

Richard said, "We've got all the time in the world, okay?"

Sophie hunched her shoulders and shrank into herself. Her thoughts whirred in their own direction. She envisioned the bright green foliage of the rainforest, the flights of colorful birds, and realized that their idyllic magic was lost to her. Her place of serenity was ruined by the specter of that strange man, encroaching and threatening her.

Her thoughts drifted to a vision of herself as a little girl, curled tightly in bed before it was time to sleep. Still in her shorts and t-shirt from the day, clutching her favorite stuffed doll. Parents gone for the night, creating that same feeling of loneliness, of loss.

Why do I feel loneliness? she asked, tinged with guilt. That was not how being attacked felt. Where was the dread? The desperation? She reflected – the dread must fade over time. But the loneliness – that remained a permanent burden. A piece of joy robbed from her.

She blinked and noticed a shallow hole in the stone wall of the building that now housed The Pirate's Rest. A building built two centuries ago, during a time when pirates attacked and killed. The crater was likely from a pirate cannon ball. Perhaps erasing a life those many years past. She'd never noticed it before.

Richard set his glass on the table and looked at her, his eyes understanding, as always.

"It happened this morning," she began.

9

He nodded and she continued, "I was walking in the bush to the east of the Coxon compound in a hanging valley in the mountains. It contains a rainforest, with lovely birds and lush green vegetation. I'd been there briefly a couple times before and I always follow the same path, a deer track. It's always been peaceful and, well, special."

Her mouth went dry and she took a sip of beer. She described the creepy stalking and the initial attack, and noticed Richard's expression turn dark. She said, "This man appeared. He came at me with his pointed knife, I charged – "

"You what?"

"I charged him. To mess up his timing. It was my only choice."

"I don't know whether to praise you or tell you you're nuts."

"I learned it in a karate class. It almost worked."

Richard took her hand. "Don't go walking in the deep woods alone. Promise me."

"Not there, that's for sure."

"I mean anywhere in the deep woods. Pirates are with us today."

"I know. You tell me the stories. Jeeze."

He squeezed her hand. "They are low-lifes. They kill people. And not just on boats."

She pulled her hand away. "God, Richard, I know. But this is St. Mark. Remote. Who'd ever find it?"

"That guy did. I'm serious. Everyone on this island loves you to pieces. Me most of all."

"I'm not a little girl, you know."

"Damn it, you've got to understand."

She crossed her arms. He didn't seem so understanding now. "So that means I stay in town or at the Coxons' and get an escort to walk between the two places?"

"No. I'm not saying you can't take care of yourself—under normal conditions. Hell, most men don't have the skills or courage to do what you did this morning. But what if there had been two of them? Or if he ambushed you? Or had a gun?"

"Hmph."

"Just stay away from the most deserted places. And let someone know where you're going."

"Like you do?"

He raised hands in mock surrender. "Okay, I'm sorry. I'm acting like a big brother. I know you'll take care. I'm worried, that's all. That's what people who love each other do."

She sighed. "For now, I only need you to listen to me so I can get this thing out of my system. I have to talk it out, okay? Then I can hear about the future."

He squeezed her hand again, gently, and let go. "Okay, deal. Do you want to tell me again?"

"Not now. I'm hungry."

After a gobbled-up dinner, Sophie drained her second glass of beer and peered at Richard. "I really need to be with you tonight."

He gave her his brotherly smile. Way different from his horny-sailor smile. He understood.

They held hands up the mountain path behind town and entered his bungalow.

He lit a kerosene lantern. "I got an invitation from Mike Stiles, inviting us for lunch tomorrow. Would you like that? You could talk with Anika."

"I don't know. I'm kind of a mess."

"She might help you sort things out. Mike says she's a good listener."

Sophie murmured, "Okay."

He went into the bedroom, leaving her alone in the kitchen. The memories returned, making her feel adrift, totally without control. Like being squashed underwater by her first ocean wave, tumbling beneath its massive surge. That man had controlled her, had stopped her tranquil ramble through nature as surely as that wave had destroyed her carefree wading.

She never managed to turn the tables on the wave – or that man. He maintained control, even though he had no right. Why did she think of this, and not of fear? She had no idea. The feeling came and settled in, welcome or not. Where did this leave her?

Should she accept that certain people could snatch control from her? No, that was a lame excuse to surrender. Well, how about – anger? That was a foreign emotion for Sophie, but now became a spark that blossomed into a flame. *Anger can motivate me to fight the stranger.*

Yes, that felt right.

Through the jalousies, she caught the glimmer of a lantern being lit inside one of the other homes. It felt like a sign.

CHAPTER 4

His watch vibrated silently and he awoke, remaining still on top of his sleeping bag, listening to the rainforest noises. After a minute, he rose, drew his knife, its white bone handle familiar and comforting, and checked the camp perimeter. Daylight was fading, causing him to move even more carefully than usual, burning up valuable time.

Satisfied there were no trespassers, he packed his night vision goggles and two packs of field rations, and filled his canteen from the creek. On his way out of the valley, he set three telltales in the form of vines strung across the deer tracks closest to his camp.

Each was supported several inches above the ground by small branches, as if having fallen naturally from above. If an intruder upset the vines in any way, he would know.

As he trotted up the steep path to the valley rim, he reviewed his immediate goal. Simple, really – determine the daily routine of Drake and of the girl. The chore could take several days, but was necessary. *Know your target, where he will be most vulnerable. Wait. And strike.*

His ultimate goal was to recover what was his—held by Richard Drake. But first things first. Tonight, he planned to wait on the mountain behind the town and observe.

He figured everyone on the island passed through the town, especially Drake, because he was a charter captain and moored his sailboat in the local harbor. At least, that's what his website indicated. The girl might be more difficult to locate. He didn't know her habits. She might only come into town every few days. But he was a patient man. A sniper.

In a little over an hour, after sunset, out of breath and sweating, he arrived at a spot with a view of the town and the bay. He settled amid the tall grass in an indentation that hid most of him from view. A single bush provided additional cover.

He could have sat upright and much more comfortably, with his chest and head above the grass, still invisible in the nearly total darkness. But he was a careful man. He hunkered down, set out his gear, and made his initial scan through gaps in the grass with night-vision goggles.

He examined the three stone buildings in a row and the wooden building off to the left. In his first half hour he spotted three people. Each made their way to one of the small cottages that dotted the hill between him and the town.

At the end of the next hour, he settled in for a long, boring night. But a door opened and shut in the building marked 'Pirate's Rest Bar and Grille.' A man and woman exited, waving good-bye to someone inside. The couple appeared completely anonymous, an average man, average woman.

The night breeze brought snippets of conversation to him. They came closer, apparently aiming for a cottage to his right. For several long seconds, light from one of the other cottages shone on their faces.

God! It was him!

Richard Drake, that gung-ho asshole from Afghanistan. His freaking target. He couldn't believe his luck. He focused on his face. Yep, even in the green hue of the NVG, Drake's features were easily identifiable.

Hmm. Who was that next to him? Jeeze! The girl! He took a deep breath and mentally patted himself on the back.

Great. I'll be Outta this shit hole in another day. Two at most.

CHAPTER 5

Richard untangled himself from the sheets, pulled on shorts and t-shirt, and padded into the kitchen. Through the open window, he surveyed beyond the harbor, where whitecaps dotted the dark blue Caribbean. Down the mountain from his bungalow, toward town, a dog barked.

The scene normally cheered him. Not today, with a damned stranger loose on the island. The situation was ticking time bomb. The man was aggressive and reckless, more full of anger than guile, at least when he encountered Sophie.

Would he be satisfied with his privacy in the valley or would be venture out and spread his anger? Did he feel safe or threatened? Would he decide to stalk Sophie, to attempt to murder her, as he had on that path? *Assume the worst*, Richard decided. He'll strike again, this time outside the valley, and soon. Today? Hell, maybe this morning.

Well, whatever, he and Sophie needed to eat breakfast. He glanced at the bedroom door. Heard noises. He turned to his cooking and rustled up coffee, bacon, and eggs.

Sophie wandered in, dressed in one of his shirts. Mussed blond hair, saucy smile, and those blue eyes. He pushed worries aside and hugged her. She hugged back and kissed him, longer than usual for a morning greeting.

She asked, "Did you get any sleep last night?"

"A little. Someone had me in a pretty strong wrestling grip, with her arms and legs."

"Sorry."

"Did it help?"

She grinned. "Lots. You make me feel safe. I needed that. Um. How hungry are you?"

He cocked his head.

She traced her finger slowly, deliberately, down his chest, "Like, not eggs, like – "

He felt a surge in his stomach and elsewhere. "Is that your answer?"

She looked below his waist and sniggered. "How do you do that so fast?"

"Magic," he said, as he guided her back to bed.

*   *   *

George looked like he'd been at work for hours when Richard and Sophie stopped by Coxon's Boat Works. It was the only industry on the island and arguably the only place in the world from which a person could order an authentic Tortola sloop, the graceful sailboat that Virgin Islanders had traditionally used to transport people and goods from place to place.

George was painting the hull of a small-sized version of the vessel. He was Richard's best friend, the unofficial mayor of St. Mark, and descendent of the original pirate captain, John Coxon, who'd retired on the island with his crew in the late seventeenth century. George was burly and quiet, with high cheekbones and hints of Arawak and Africa in his build.

"Is that it?" Sophie asked.

George gazed at the smooth hull. "Yep, getting her ready."

"Jenny's birthday party," murmured Richard.

George said, with a twinkle in his eye, "It'll be a surprise. I told Jenny that, of course, we're having her party on the actual day of her birthday, but the museum folks said they'll be in the Caribbean on that date, and it would save a trip if they could take delivery. She said that was fine and even volunteered to teach them how to sail her." He nodded toward Richard. "My accomplice here will arrange for a couple of St. Thomas people Jenny doesn't know to pose as the museum representatives. It's all worked out."

Sophie moved to the bow and looked aft, admiring the graceful shape of the hull. "She's beautiful. Worthy of a museum." She grinned at George. "Or a wonderful daughter. She'll love it."

16

"I think so," George said. "She did lots of the work herself. She has much more interest in the Boat Works than Michael. Probably take over when I retire."

"I have a favor to ask."

George nodded. "Sure."

"I'm going with Richard to visit Mike and Anika in St. Thomas this morning, sort of a last-minute invitation. Uncle John's not back yet and I'm minding his store."

"Ah, you need someone there for the day. I'll have Michael run home and ask Maren to take it. She'll enjoy talking to all the shoppers, catching up on news."

"Thanks, George."

"Sure. Are you coming for dinner tonight?"

"Yes. We'll be back way before dark, right Richard?"

He nodded. "Late afternoon, I'm thinking."

"Okay, and you're invited as well," George said to Richard.

Richard smiled. "Sounds good."

Twenty minutes later, they departed the small harbor, CAPRICE's hull slicing through Caribbean rollers. Both of them sat in the cockpit, Richard at the wheel, aft, and Sophie forward on the port side, tucked into her usual spot.

They caught a southeast breeze, this morning blowing about twenty knots. The boat sped around the west end of Jost Van Dyke and entered Pillsbury Sound, with St. Thomas to starboard, St. John on the port side. The sound was rough, as usual, and CAPRICE pitched in the steep seas.

As if by agreement, they avoided talking about Sophie's episode the previous day. She'd told Richard the story again back at his bungalow. He'd listened and asked questions only if he needed clarification. He gave no advice.

He noticed shadows under her eyes and felt sure she'd slept poorly the previous night. He was heartened when she gazed up at the white clouds, turned her face to the wind, and even smiled a bit.

He wanted to give her an opportunity to feel normal, to continue the good mood of the morning. Let happy memories start nudging others aside. He checked the tell-tails on the main, pointed the boat into the wind a little, and listened with satisfaction to the hum of the stainless-steel standing rigging.

Unbidden, thoughts came to him of the violent stranger. His chest tightened and a voice in his mind snarled, *Find him and kill him.* That was a Marine's solution. It was totally acceptable in combat against a national enemy, but not here. Not in civilian life.

Besides, the stranger could be deranged, to be treated with caution but also with care. In any case, Richard's way forward must be to find the man and turn him over to the police. Let the law determine the appropriate outcome. But he must be found quickly, before he harmed Sophie or someone else.

Or set his sights on the judge, Richard reflected with dread. Providing security for the man was the reason Richard had come to St. Mark. To say his charter business was a front would be an exaggeration, but not by much. The business took him all over the US and British Virgin Islands, where he nurtured contacts with other charter captains, marina attendants, and police. He kept his eyes and ears open for rumors and suspicious visitors and formed the outer ring of the judge's security. Two Spanish special forces police formed the inner ring, and the three of them teamed up during times of threat.

So far, the intruder appeared focused on Sophie and not the judge. Also, the judge was presiding on a case in The Hague, so was in no danger from the stranger. When he returned to his compound on St. Mark, Richard would brief him and his security detail.

Suddenly impatient for this day to be over, Richard wondered if taking the time to visit to his friends was a mistake. Maybe he should be in the valley right now instead of giving the stranger more time to dig in, reconnoiter the valley, and gain the advantage.

A rogue wave rammed the port bow, jerking Richard out of his reverie. Spray flew aft, drenching them both and flooding the cockpit. Sophie yelped, Richard swore. Then they looked at each other and laughed out loud. She rose in the pitching boat, made her way aft and plopped down next to him.

She kissed him on the lips and out of the blue declared, "Sometimes, you're just the sweetest."

They rounded the east end of St. Thomas and sailed along its southern coast, past homes, hotels, and bars on the water and perched on the steep mountains. After they passed a tiny island called Green Cay, Richard tacked into Frenchman's Bay. A hundred feet from the beach, he turned into the wind. Sophie lowered the flapping mainsail and then scampered forward and lowered the jib.

She moved with her usual athletic grace, but her expression said that she'd been thinking about what happened in the valley. Richard wondered if they should have talked more about it – maybe he shouldn't have assumed she'd dwell only on the beauty of the islands. He shrugged inwardly, rose, and moved forward to set the anchor.

He gazed up the mountain to the house where the Stiles lived, and he waved. He'd been there before and knew Mike kept a telescope on the wide south porch of the main house. He'd be checking on who had just sailed into his private bay. Pretty girls in swimsuits were fine, quiet couples as well, but noisy folks or those looking to 'visit' the property, he would run off, especially at night. At gun point. Yep, piracy was alive and well in the islands.

They swam from CAPRICE to the beach, holding bags with a change of clothes above the water, and they hiked a trail straight up the mountain to the Stiles' home. Mike and Anika met them in a parking area, and Anika guided them up stone stairs to a shaded patio located between the main house and the kitchen.

Richard and Sophie showered and changed and they all met back at the patio, under its vine-covered arbor. Sophie gazed down into a deep valley, then off left to where the valley opened onto the bay and the sparkling Caribbean.

She smiled from ear to ear. "I love this view! And your house, Anika."

"Thank you," Anika said modestly, gesturing for all to sit at a table decorated with flowers and set for four with elegant Danish stainless-steel ware and tall glasses of iced tea. "I'll show you around after lunch."

They talked of island news during lunch and then the women cleared the table and exited to the kitchen. Richard grinned when he heard their conversation, more animated than during lunch. *Good, they're becoming friends.* To Mike he said, "I'm thinking we should take a walk, maybe into the valley, along the beach."

"Yeah, catch up on things, like we talked about on the phone."

CHAPTER 6

He awoke as dawn turned the surrounding trees from shadows to shades of gray. Just like in Afghanistan, the sun was opening a freaking new can of worms in a place better left forgotten. He swallowed a curse and turned to his morning rituals, checked his perimeter, and started a tiny fire, made of the driest twigs he could find to minimize smoke.

After breakfast of coffee and beef jerky, he set his task for the day – establish a base camp and a backup, and divide his gear between the two. The camps had to be secure, with a view of their surroundings. There must be no surprises from lurking trespassers.

His temporary camp was on the east side of the creek that bisected the valley from north to south. He stayed on that side, moving south, in the same direction as the babbling water, the sheer valley wall off to his left. Just himself, dripping water, the cawing birds, and chattering insects. God, the place was noisy.

At length, he heard the sound of a waterfall. He approached the creek, now ten feet across, flowing quickly, then working itself up into a rage as it entered the rock-walled gorge. He leaned over the water to see past encroaching tree limbs and survey the tumbling rapids.

The sides of the gorge were sheer. Not much chance of getting out that way. A person would have to ride the broiling water and drop off the waterfall at the other end. He considered. *What an excellent place to dispose of Drake.*

He narrowed his eyes, thinking. He could gain the advantage in a fight, push him into the rapids here, and the water would sweep him away so quickly he'd be unable to regain the shore before entering the gorge. And then, over the fall, an 'accident,' as if he slipped into the creek.

He walked upstream until he found a tree to bridge the creek and carefully crossed to the west side. He advanced to the valley wall and followed it northward. After half an hour, he found what he was looking for – a twenty-foot high boulder that protruded from the wall.

It appeared impossible to climb except in one place, on the south side, at the joint between boulder and valley wall. The joint contained horizontal and angled cracks, forming a sort of ladder into which a man could place his boots and grip with his hands.

He climbed easily and reached the top of the nearly flat boulder. He sat back from the edge, invisible from below. It was supremely defensible. Only one person at a time could ascend the rocky ladder and his head would be exposed when he reached the top. Easy pickings with a pistol.

But to remain out of sight from those on the valley floor he must remain low. When he stood, he was exposed from the waist up. His camo jungle outfit enabled him blend for short periods, sufficient to rise and quickly check his surroundings for intruders.

He decided to make the boulder his backup camp. The only drawback of the place was that options for escape were limited. The gorge was too steep to exit from the south, effectively cornering him in the south quarter of the valley. He must look further for a viable base camp.

He turned and for the first time noticed a cave leading into the valley wall. He entered, and found it large enough for a man to stand, deep enough to shelter from the rain. Water dripped from several places in the ceiling, puddling on a floor composed of rock partially covered with earth. Green moss lined parts of the walls. There were nooks and crannies perfect for hiding enough food for several days.

At the mouth of the cave, he saw evidence of a fire. He looked around for other signs of visitors but found only a small stack of twigs, probably for the fire. He kicked at the black ashes and decided the fire had been dormant for years.

He drew his knife and stepped to the back of the cave and peered into the gloom. The passage narrowed and decreased in height, causing him to stoop. Ten feet in, the light was almost non-existent. He paused then backed out. Without his flashlight he was unwilling to risk disturbing an animal or tumbling into a hole in the floor.

He descended the rocky ladder to the valley floor and continued north. Along the way, he saw two possible sites for his base camp but upon close inspection judged neither was up to par. Nor were there other options on the west wall or the short north wall. Not until almost a quarter of the way south along the east wall did he spot a promising site.

It was a rock ledge, a little higher on the valley wall than the boulder of his backup camp. As with that other camp, this one was well below the rainforest canopy. There was no natural ladder, but he was able to use saplings growing out of the valley wall for support, and readily climbed up.

When he reached the ledge, he had to squeeze between a growth of bushes that surrounded the perimeter and was pleasantly surprised to find a flat clearing within. He stood at the center of the clearing. The bushes grew about four feet high, so he could sit and even move around without being seen from below. Narrow gaps in the foliage allowed him to surveil the surrounding forest.

He sat on his haunches, swallowed water from his canteen and considered. There was plenty of space to lay out a sleeping bag and a cook stove and other gear. There was no cave, but that was okay. He had a poncho in case it rained.

As far as options for escape, he'd discovered two steep paths connecting the rainforest with the surrounding mountains and their dry trees and bushes. The nearest was across the creek and north, near enough to use as an escape route but not so close that intruders would accidently bump into his camp. The other one, used by the girl, was further south along that same west wall.

CHAPTER 7

Sophie helped Anika while the guys took a walk in the valley. The kitchen was large and modern, with a fine stove, oven, fridge, and large freezer. Unlike the Coxons' home, the Stiles had electric power. But windows and doors were the same – wooden jalousies – and, like on St. Mark, all were open to the island breeze.

"I think your home is a perfect blend," Sophie said, as Anika washed and she dried. "It's modern but also traditional. I'll bet your original ancestors would love it, too."

"They'd sure like the refrigeration. In those days, they had to get the milk to town before the day got too hot. There was a coastal road – more of a track really – so at least they didn't have to climb all the steep hills, which were muddy during times of rain until a few decades ago when the main roads were finally paved.

Anyway, they'd love being able to store the milk cold, and I'm glad you like the place. There, that's the last plate." She beamed at Sophie. "I'm glad you came. I love Mike to pieces, but sometimes I need a woman to talk with, you know?"

"Oh, yes. Men just don't get relationships."

"And hair and styles."

"Or jewelry. I like your bracelet."

"Thanks. It's gold and came from my grandmother. She bought it in Denmark when my parents and I went back for a visit. I was only five or six." Anika jangled the bracelet, her expression wistful. "I remember her wearing it all the time."

"Well, it's gorgeous. Oh, I wanted to make sure you guys were coming to Jenny's birthday party."

"Ah yes," Anika said, giving the sink and counter a final dash with her sponge. "We sure are. We're riding over with two of Richard's friends. Partners in a law firm on the island. They'll pretend to be from the museum that's supposed to be getting the boat."

"Good. Maren's looking forward to you staying the night. You'll be in the cottage they're letting me use. I'll stay with Richard in town."

"We can't wait," Anika said, and she led the way back to the patio and gestured toward the main house. "Would you like to take a look around?"

"Oh, yes! I guess that's another 'woman thing.' Exploring houses."

"It bores Mike to death."

"Richard, too. Though he'll spend a whole day poking around inside boats."

Anika said over her shoulder as she guided Sophie into the main house, "Mike would do the same with military tanks, I'm sure."

Sophie entered a large room with a grass-mat floor covering and comfortable Danish chairs and couches, two standing lamps, and a coffee table. To her left was a dining table of teak, again Danish, with seating for eight.

"This is where we usually have our dinners," Anika said, "especially if the weather is rainy or windy."

She led the way out of the main room to the master bedroom and bath, then down a hallway with clothes closets on either side, to an office. From the office she stepped onto a wide, shaded porch, where a breeze ruffled their hair. There were lounge chairs, a telescope on a tripod, and a small bar. In front of the porch lay two ten-by-ten-foot lawns, bordered by short hedges and flowers.

Beyond that was a concrete deck, which on second look turned out to be the arched top of a cistern. They walked out and stood on the rough concrete, with the valley, bay, and Caribbean far below.

Sophie caught her breath. "What a view!"

"We have morning coffee on the porch and admire the sea, and at night we often bring air mattresses out on the cistern and lie down to watch the sky and count falling stars."

Sophie turned to her friend. "Aren't we are lucky to be living in the islands?"

"We are. I don't miss the bustle of the States at all. Of course, I've only been to big cities to visit, never to live there. It's the same with Denmark – only short visits. Our families have lived here since the dairy farm was built."

"Wow. I grew up in Florida and practically lived in the ocean. But to be on an island where the pace is civilized. It's the best."

Anika laughed. "And your St. Mark is even more laid back than St. Thomas. We're frenetic at times in town. With several thousand tourists arriving from cruise ships, the place is a crush and the store where I work is amazingly crowded."

"I can see why you like living here in the countryside. You can recharge."

Anika showed Sophie two guest cottages, much like the one where she stayed with the Coxons, then they returned to the front porch. They sat side-by-side in lounge chairs, with glasses of cool Pinot Grigio. Sophie felt comfortable with Anika, who'd helped her in the past during a terrible part of her life. They had lunch together in town several times, when Richard took her along before a charter.

They talked about this and that, and by the second glass of Pinot, the conversation became more personal. Sophie wondered if her friend would talk about island magic, but the conversation turned to other topics and quite naturally ended up with Anika describing how she and Mike met and the scary adventure that followed.

"Right here," she said at the conclusion of her tale, "on the porch."

Sophie caught her breath. It all looked very peaceful – the house and the land. Mike and Sophie. "To think you both have been through all that."

Anika nodded solemnly. "We're glad it's behind us. As is your experience with your ex-boyfriend."

"Cliff Webb," murmured Sophie, shutting her mind to the fear and violence of those awful days. But unfortunately, she had other concerns now.

They sipped their wine in silence for a minute before Sophie said, "Anika, something new has happened. A new adventure, or rather, another serious problem. Something like what we just talked about, I'm afraid."

Anika's eyes turned sympathetic. "Mike told me Richard mentioned something on the sat phone this morning. He said you may be preoccupied when you arrived. Your expression several times at lunch, Sophie – you looked concerned."

Sophie gathered her thoughts. Took a fortifying sip of wine, and recounted the events of the previous morning. "Richard thinks it's some guy trying to drop out of sight. Probably not dangerous if we don't push him. Anyway, being Richard, he's planning to do a little 'recon,' as he says."

"I wouldn't want to be in the stranger's shoes. Richard is very protective of you. I don't know if you have noticed that. He respects your ability and your courage and treats you as an equal – but he can't help wanting to look after you." She poured the last of the wine. "Come to think of it, my Mike is the same."

"We've found two good men."

They clinked their glasses and sipped.

"I like this wine," Sophie said.

"Yeah. And it gets better the more you drink."

Anika looked thoughtful. "The thing is, yes, they respect our skills but, when it comes down to it, the two of them will always be — "

"Macho men." Sophie laughed. "And they'll remain that way their whole lives. Which means — "

"Protecting their *wimmin* is pri one."

"Hoo-ah!" they said in unison.

CHAPTER 8

Richard followed Mike down the steep road to the valley. Halfway down, they passed a small gray cottage perched on the left side of the road.

"Your original home away from home," Richard remarked, remembering Mike's tales of his introduction to the estate.

Mike glanced at the structure. "Yeah, brings back memories. Mostly bad, but a few good ones, like meeting Anika. Though at first she wasn't happy to see a squatter on her daddy's place, even though they lived in town. I must have seemed like an unwelcome intruder in Anika's mind, the way Sophie sees that stranger."

Richard rubbed his chin as they continued toward the inland end of a valley. "Except you didn't stalk her with evil intentions."

"True. More like she stalked me. You know the stories."

"Yep. In the end, she couldn't help herself. You were so dang handsome and manly she had to fall in love with you."

Mike laughed. He guided Richard down and left, through the lush valley. A deer peeked from the underbrush and bounded away, soundless and graceful.

They walked beneath a great tree with massive trunk and limbs, full of birds that squawked and took flight. The shade felt good. Then they were back in the open, the house high on the mountain, looking like a fortress with its white-washed walls.

They paused when they reached the beach, the sea breeze smelling salty and fresh. To their right, black rocks and boulders defined the west end of the bay. To their left, the beach stretched a couple hundred yards to the east. Between was crystal clear water, rippled by the wind, turning shades of ever-darker turquoise as it deepened and met the deep blue of the Caribbean.

Mike grunted, looked up at the house, sketched a wave. "They'll be looking at us."

Richard nodded, followed his friend's gaze, and caught himself smiling at the two women standing on the porch. God, he was glad he had Sophie. He figured he'd propose one starry night. Not now, though. She wasn't ready. He understood.

"Take a walk up the beach?" he suggested.

They strolled on the sand, beneath squawking seagulls. Land crabs scrabbled amid palm trees. CAPRICE rocked peacefully at anchor, her shrouds clanging in time with her motion in gentle swells.

"A cold beer would taste mighty fine about now," Mike drawled.

"Good thing we're trained to ignore being thirsty, tough as we are."

"Macho combat vets."

"Yup," Mike said. "By the way, am I imagining things or was there an elephant in the room at lunch?"

"Not imagining," Richard responded. "It was what I skimmed over during our conversation this morning. Only had time for the bare bones. Wanted to fill you in on the details when we both had plenty of time. Privacy, too."

"This happened on St. Mark?"

"Yeah, yesterday morning, just east of the Coxon place, in an isolated valley. A rainforest. I've never been there. Didn't know we had rainforests on St. Mark."

"So, it started when she heard someone on her path?"

"Right, approaching her, sneaky like, appearing suddenly and charging her. Tried to kill her with a knife."

"Kill her? I thought he only wanted to bully her."

"Nope. He was out for blood."

"Why the hell? Did she know him?"

"Never saw him before. She doesn't have a clue why he attacked. She said he was dressed in military fatigues and had a big knife with a bone handle. She's damned lucky she got away. Trouble is, I don't think it's over."

"You're telling me this guy is still loose on your island?"

"Yeah."

Mike's face flushed. "Holy fuck! What the hell are you doing here? Why haven't you called the police? The Army?"

Richard laughed "Whoa, Mike. You and I both know police and most Army units would be useless tracking someone trained in jungle fighting. I'm going after him, pure and simple, and I wanted to talk my plans through with you first."

"Are you sure he's so skilled? He sounds to me like a wanna-be dressed in military gear who almost got his ass handed to him by Sophie."

"Don't believe it. She got away by the skin of her teeth. She surprised him, ruined his initial moves. About the time he got his shit in one sock, she took off. Good thing she's a runner and he's not."

"You really think he's got jungle skills?"

"Listening to how Sophie described his attack, and his quick reversal of her defenses, I think so. Plus, he got to the island and into the valley undetected."

"Huh. What are your thoughts on getting rid of him?"

"First off, I need to get the lay of the land. I'm a desert guy. I do just fine in a place like Afghanistan. But this valley is the next thing to a freaking jungle. It's a totally new environment for me, all close-in vegetation, claustrophobic compared to the wide-open spaces of the desert and mountains."

"So, first you do a little recon."

"Yeah, nice and careful. Look through that valley, get a feel for what's there, how to move quietly, how to hide and how this guy might hide. I'll also be on the lookout for signs, you know, look for disturbed ground, broken branches, footprints."

"Okay, here's what I think. He'll have a place where he's either well hidden, like in a copse of trees and bushes, or in a cave, or up on a spur off the valley wall."

"You figure his priorities are to stay out of sight while being able to see other folks who come through?"

"Yup," Mike said, "that's how I'd do it. Hide among the bushes, but have a tree or rock handy where I could climb up and search the surrounding area. That's probably how he discovered Sophie. Gotta be careful, man. He could be packing firepower."

"Okay, that makes sense. So to be safe, we'll assume he's trained in evasion and attack. Especially attack."

"Yep. Sounds as though he's on a mission of some kind. Right now, I'd say he's guarding his perimeter, setting up defensive positions. When he feels settled in, he'll venture out to do whatever he's come to do. Maybe as early as tomorrow, no way to say. You've gotta get your ass in gear, buddy. What were you, Marine Force Recon?"

"Yes, and we never jumped feet first. We took the 'recon' part seriously. Studied intel photos and got up close and personal with the terrain and the threats."

"Well, you've gotten your threat assessment from Sophie, and I agree that this guy's gotta be taken seriously."

"Right," Richard said, "now I'll recon the terrain."

"And keep an eye peeled for him while you're doing that?"

Richard gave him a look.

"Just saying. You gotta move fast. Get to him while he's still figuring out the valley and planning how to defend himself. Once he's dug in, your problems become multiplied. Think of Iwo Jima. Battleships out the wazoo blasting the place, with those Japanese hunkered down underground nice and safe."

"I'll go in tomorrow, early."

"Armed, Richard. Assume he's gunning for you. Maybe he's just some poor crazy. But crazy folks can be unpredictable, dangerous. Until you know why he's lurking out there, threatening people, you have to expect the worst. If he's got a combat knife and training, he's probably got fire power. You want a little company? I could use the excitement."

"God, Mike, the guy's probably just a low-life. But thanks. I'll call you if things get touchy."

Mike looked him in the eye. "I do not want to lose you – or Sophie. Oh, one more thing. If he stays more than a few days, he may come rummaging around people's houses and in that general store you have on the island. Food is bulky and heavy. He can only have carried so much with him. When it's gone, he'll need to restock."

They walked a few steps, then Mike broke the silence, his voice grim. "Sorry, but I've got to add to your bad news."

"What?"

"It doesn't affect us, but I wanted to let you know. Seems like a couple of Afghanistan vets died mysterious deaths, each appearing to be accidental but too coincidental as far as I'm concerned. One in your Marine unit, the other in a nearby Army unit where I know a few of the guys."

"Damn, that's mighty close to home. Did you get names?"

"Not yet. I'm gathering dribs and drabs from guys I know. I'll keep you posted."

CHAPTER 9

Sophie and Richard departed Frenchman's Bay on CAPRICE. They waved at Anika and Mike, plainly visible on the cistern, waving back.

Richard turned the boat to port, into rolling blue Caribbean swells. Frenchman's bay and Green Cay dropped astern. Buck Island with its abandoned lighthouse squatted a couple miles ahead to the right.

Sophie curled up in the forward port corner of the cockpit, enjoying the glow from the Pinot, and even more, the closeness of a deepening friendship with Anika. Sophie sensed in her a kindred spirit.

Anika was born and raised on St. Thomas – definitely an island girl, with solid roots back many generations. Yet, she had opened her arms to Sophie, a newcomer, starting with only an introduction back when she was in trouble. Today had been their first opportunity to simply sit back and talk. No interruptions. No deadlines.

"A penny for your thoughts?" Richard asked.

"Wow, there's an old expression."

"Ha, you think it should be a quarter these days?"

"How about a dollar?"

He grinned.

"No," she said. "Not for my thoughts. They're definitely not worth a dollar."

"Well, I'll take them for free. Oh, and how about adding a kiss?"

"That *is* free," Sophie said. She maneuvered closer and snuggled in for a deep kiss. "Mmm. You taste like beer."

"Sorry." He massaged her shoulder tenderly, like he meant business.

She glanced back at the open hatchway into the salon. With nice, comfy beds. Hmm. "Too bad," she whispered into his ear.

"We could anchor," he suggested hopefully.

"Someone would see. How about tonight?"

"It's a date." She kissed him again and slid back to her spot. God, he was a hunk. And what a kisser. She loved how he lingered, took his time, all his attention on her. She caught him looking her over.

Funny, she thought, *the breeze isn't as cool as it was a minute ago.* "Is it hot, or just me?"

He laughed. "It's you. You're a hot number, Sophie. Oops, hang on!"

The boat rose, dove steeply into a trough, and slammed into the next swell. Spray exploded in white sheets on either side of the bow and blew back, dousing them both.

"So much for heat," she said.

He grinned. She looked down at her soaking swim suit. "I'll be right back." Down below, she toweled off, changed into the dry top and shorts she'd worn for lunch, and returned.

"Aren't you cold?" she asked.

"A little. I'll dry off." His tone had changed, as if the cold spray had shifted his thinking. Yes, his expression, his eyes, looked somber and introspective.

"Did you and Mike have a good walk?" she said, giving him an opening to share what she suspected they'd discussed.

"Yeah. Pretty good. We talked about the stranger in the rain forest. Mike volunteered to help out."

"He's a Ranger, right?"

"Yes, and he was posted to Panama for a short time, where got experience patrolling their rain forests. Which is more than I have. I'm a desert rat."

"Will you call on him?"

"Not yet," he said, which was what she'd expected. *Men.* Always wanted to solve their own problems. Richard was no exception, though he was opening up more than when they'd first met.

"I'll call him if things get dangerous," he said, as if reading her thoughts. "He's a good man under pressure according Graham

Walters. Turns out we both still work for Graham on a fairly regular basis."

"Do you and Mike think this man is dangerous?"

"We agreed that we need to be very careful around him. He could have mental problems, or maybe he's hiding from the law."

Richard spun the wheel, turning the boat port. They entered Pillsbury Sound, with St. Thomas still on their left, and now St. John on their right, up ahead.

"Well," she said, "I had a good talk with Anika. That's what I was thinking about back there. She listened to my story about the stranger in the rain forest. She's a good listener. Also, a good talker."

"I think we've got a couple of special friends."

She nodded in agreement. "Didn't you say she was magical or something?"

"Yes, it's a side she's private about. I don't know many details. It has to do with Jumbee magic. 'Jumbee' is what the locals call Zombies, the local dialect. Jumbees are grouchy spirits that play tricks on the living. Some are less grouchy than others."

Sophie put her hand to her mouth, eyes wide. "My gosh, Richard. She's a Jumbee?"

He shrugged. "I wouldn't say that, exactly. But back in her ancestry, there's Jumbee blood. She's said a few things about her father, and mentioned that she didn't fall far from the tree."

"But she's totally nice, so sweet."

"That's who she really is, as far as I can tell. I've only heard a little from Mike. He cracked a joke once about not getting her mad or I'd find myself surrounded by toads. Apparently, she didn't approve of him when they first met. Something about him squatting on her family's land."

"But he was watching for drug smugglers. You told me the story."

"Yeah, well, sparks flew at first."

"I wish she'd talk about it. Sounds fascinating."

"She'll tell you, just give her time."

"Yeah, little by little. Today we shared more than when we'd had lunch together."

"It felt right – you know, comfortable?"

"Yes, and the same with you and Mike?"

"Pretty much. After we talked about your encounter, he told me about several mysterious deaths of Army and Marine vets who'd served in Afghanistan and returned home, started civilian lives."

"Mysterious? How?"

"He didn't know details but he promised to keep me posted. We agreed that something doesn't seem right. The deaths at first appeared to be accidents, but further investigation indicates there could have been foul play."

"Like someone murdered them?"

He looked at her for a few moments, eyes grave, as if turning things over in his mind. Finally, he nodded in an absent-minded way. As if he were putting things together, or at least trying to. And what he came up with bothered him.

She sensed Richard's protective shield close around her. That should have made her feel safe, but it didn't. She glanced at him, a little crease of worry in his forehead. She realized she was becoming protective of her protector.

They'd passed Jost Van Dyke and St. Mark lay ahead, the harbor entrance a half mile distant.

"Look," she said, pointing toward a white ribbon of water high in the mountains to the right of the harbor.

"What is it? Looks like a waterfall."

"It is. From the creek that runs down the center of the valley, fed by the rain forest. It starts as a brook at the north end of the forest and builds to a creek and then rapids when it's forced through a gorge at the south end."

"It's beautiful," he said. "I guess I've seen it before, but never really noticed." He continued, his tone brooding, "So that's the hanging valley, nestled half way up the mountains. Looks like it's to the east of the Coxon place."

"Yup, pretty close too. About a ten-minute walk to the valley wall, where you get on a twisty, steep path to reach the floor."

As she spoke, the feelings of the previous morning returned, sending goosebumps prickling her arms.

And it might get worse, she reflected.

Probably will get worse.

She hugged herself.

CHAPTER 10

He spent the morning and early afternoon lugging gear from hiding places near his temporary camp to his base and backup camps. The work kept his body occupied, but his mind wandered.

He thought about his encounter with the woman the previous morning and shook his head in disgust. Attacking her was mistake, not at all reflective of his sniper's code. He should have stayed hidden, let her pass. That this painfully obvious fact had lingered until now to raise its ugly head surprised him. Maybe it was the final straw.

The entire mission was becoming too much a pain in the ass, and way too personal. The solution was to kill, no doubt about that. But he much preferred killing at a distance, where he could see but not touch and smell the results of his handiwork.

Because of his blunder, someone would come searching for him. It could even be Richard. How well would the Force Recon Marine perform in the rainforest? It used to be, during Vietnam, soldiers knew the jungle. Now all they knew was the moonscape of Afghanistan. What shit holes – both places.

After a lunch of field rations and after he arranged his final load at his base camp, he looked up through gaps in the canopy and saw that the afternoon was fading to dusk. It was time to leave the valley and get into position.

On his way out of the valley, he set three telltales in the form of vines laid across the deer tracks that passed the closest to his base camp. Each was supported several inches above the ground by small branches, as if having fallen naturally from above. If an intruder upset the vines in any way, he would know and be alert to others traversing his valley.

CHAPTER 11

Sophie watched Richard pass through town on his way to change for dinner at the Coxons'. She had half an hour alone at the store. That was all the time she needed.

She walked into the store but, almost immediately, felt enveloped by a mixture of confused feelings of vulnerability, yearning, and loneliness. She drifted along the first aisle, wondering at her sudden change of mood.

When Richard was by her side and they were talking, or even when they were silent, these confused feelings hovered, but they never surfaced like. They remained at arm's length and bearable.

The hair raised on her arms, a physical sign of her conflict between past and future. *God,* it felt the same as that other time, when Cliff, her violent ex-boyfriend, had come to the island and hunted her down with vengeance on his mind. Vengeance? No, it was *murder*.

She cast back, attempting to identify and reassert whatever she had done following those dark days, to recover her balance and leave the violence behind. But nothing came to mind, and recollections of the stranger's attack and her retreat boiled in her head like a witch's brew.

Why was she so upset? She had gotten away and she had Richard to protect her. On the other hand, was it bad for her to be upset? What would Maren do, or Anika? Would they turn the tables and focus on dealing with the stranger? Maybe.

Anyway, she still felt violated and yearned for normalcy. She did have faith that the intensity of her emotions would ebb, given time. In fact, she had a plan, the thought of which brought a grim smile to her lips.

She entered the back room, straightened a couple of boxes, and smoothed an errant wrinkle in the tan blanket that covered Uncle John's bed. Other thoughts entered her mind, thoughts of action – one reason for her visiting the valley the previous morning. She had gone to search for a place where she could run and hide if the need should ever again arise.

She hoped that finding such a place would quell the constant gnawing at her spirit, a simmering feeling of desolation, of defenselessness, which she now admitted had never gone away, even after Cliff had left the picture.

She swallowed hard and reached under the bed. Felt the box, nearly too big to fit beneath the mattress, and coaxed it out, into the middle of the floor. Its FedEx colors were muted in the dimming light of late afternoon.

The box had come on the ferry, ordered almost two weeks previously and arriving at an opportune time. She peeked inside, touched the contents, felt her shoulders tense and then relax. *Maybe this will help.* Sophie closed the box and pushed it back under the bed. She stood and brushed dust from her clothes, then exited the store.

Five minutes later, even more quickly than the promised half hour, Richard appeared. He'd changed into fresh khaki shorts and t-shirt.

She kissed him. "You smell like soap."

"Is that better than beer?"

She laughed. "I'll take either one."

She pushed the front door shut and they aimed up the blacktop road, which connected the town with the compounds of the rich and famous on the North Side. After five minutes of climbing the slope, they left the town and islanders' cottages behind. Trees and bushes lined the road, boxing in the heat of the late afternoon.

They turned at an unmarked dirt track and entered the shade of old trees. To their left, the mountain continued upward to its peak in the center of the island, and on the right it dropped off toward the sea.

Sophie reached out and took Richard's hand. He smiled briefly at her. She missed their romantic banter and grabbing and touching and teasing each other about the last time they had sex, or the next time. Laughing about some silly thing one or the other said, and remarking on how deliciously good it all was.

The fun times will come again, she promised herself. She squeezed his hand and he squeezed back. *I'll bet he's thinking the same thing.*

They passed through a darkened part of the track, and Sophie stole a look over her shoulder. She glimpsed Richard's eyes, scanning the way ahead and side to side. He also checked their back trail, and their eyes met. They shared a grim smile.

The trees gave way to a grassy field, slanting upward to the Coxons' main house, a single-story structure of masonry walls with exterior stucco, painted a light pink, with a green-shuttered window to either side of the door.

The Coxons greeted them with hugs, and everyone sat on wicker chairs on the front porch. Ten-year-old Jenny presented Sophie with a glass of wine, and fourteen-year-old Michael handed Richard a frosty Tuborg.

Sophie felt the touch of the evening breeze strengthening and beginning to whisper through the surrounding trees. After a few minutes, Maren rose and she, Sophie, and Jenny walked to the kitchen, in its separate building to the left of the house. They made final dinner preparations and sent Jenny to tell the men all was ready. Everyone gathered at the long table in the great room, loaded with a fine dinner of roasted pork, sweet potatoes, and fresh fruit. George said grace.

Jenny told a story about herself and her gang of kids at the blow hole west of town. The seas had been high and everyone became fully soaked. Michael talked about the intricacies of shaping boat ribs to be even on each side and graduate smoothly in size from bow and stern to the center.

Jenny put in her two cents worth on boat design, and her big brother listened and nodded, appearing pleased she was learning the art of boat building and bemused at being upstaged. After dinner, the two of them made their escape to things more fun than gabbing with adults.

Conversation turned from St. Thomas news to the stranger lurking in the isolated valley.

"The man is a menace," Richard said. "A person could almost forgive him for spooking Sophie if he had simply asked for his privacy — to conduct a wildlife study, or something."

"Like butterflies," George said.

"Right. Butterflies. *And*, if he had met with you ahead of time, George, and explained his needs."

Maren frowned. "But — "

"Yes, *but*," Richard said. "First, he snuck in, probably landed on the North Side of the island at night. How he knew about the valley I don't have the foggiest idea. Maybe he didn't care what it was, and it simply turned out to be a hidden valley with a dense rainforest. The point is, he attacked Sophie with intent to kill." Richard looked at each of the others. "I'm going in there tomorrow morning. "

"I can show you the place," George offered quietly.

Richard gestured. "Thanks, George, but this first time I need to be alone. It's what I do. Look around. Remain invisible. I'll avoid contact with the stranger and learn the lay of the land – the creek, deer tracks, the the vegetation."

"But no contact?" Sophie asked, hearing the strain in her voice.

Richard looked at her with a small smile, but his eyes were serious. "No contact."

"Yet," said George.

"Yet," repeated Richard.

Sophie took his hand, which was calloused, strong, and dry. Hers was a sweat pit. She said, "I'm looking forward to Uncle John coming back." She made eye contact with Maren, hoping her friend would help change the subject to a happy topic.

To Sophie's relief, Maren smiled. "I do, too. He's missed – his modest ways, his smile. He's a loved fixture on the island."

Sophie nodded, and reflected that, before the attack, being alone in the store had been a comfortable time to collect her thoughts between customers.

But now it was an empty, hollow time. A time that *he* – the stranger – could choose to come and attack her again.

CHAPTER 12

After an hour of overland hiking, he was short of breath and sweltering. He arrived at his observation site on the mountain behind town. The sun had set and twilight was fading into darkness.

He lay perfectly still in the tall grass. He soon caught his breath, but with inactivity, his mind latched onto *that feeling*, a dark consciousness, borne of too many missions. Burnout, he figured. 'Sniper's disease,' the doc had said. Well, yeah, plus he'd killed a few extras, for himself. Milked the situation.

'PTSD,' they'd pronounced, which led to his medical discharge. He looked for work in New Jersey, where a buddy let him sleep on his couch for a week.

But there were few civilian jobs for snipers. Police, Secret Service, and a couple other outfits used them, but his record would nix membership in such organizations. Bland words in his fitness reports marked him as a wild cannon to those who knew the code.

Well, the Army was responsible for his condition and the Army owed him. Lucky for him, he'd realized that and made his arrangements. He was almost set.

He switched his thoughts to the rainforest, which he found to be surprisingly reminiscent of the wilds of Virginia and Louisiana. The pungent smells brought back memories of good times when he used to pole his skiff through still waters. He'd looked forward to little discoveries around the next bend, and all the while daydreamed about a cute girl in English class.

That innocent life was long gone. Since then, he'd collected new memories, bad stuff he'd tried to box up and forget. But memories tended to creep out of their boxes.

His mind conjured views of his past targets, people he'd turned into dead meat. Flies swarmed and alighted on their bodies. Buzzards tore and swallowed chunks of flesh. Dogs feasted. He guessed all that was coming back because of PTSD. Sneaky stuff, afraid to pop up during the day.

No worries. He'd clear it all up. He'd find the girl and Drake, ambush and kill them. Then disappear and leave all his nightmares behind, a free man, set for the rest of his life.

He waited. Twilight became darkness and stars shined from above. A sliver of moon appeared. Foliage turned shades of green in his night-vision goggles, looking surreal, all the world like those bodies, each with a hole in the center of the chest.

He constantly scanned down the mountain to the buildings, and to his flanks and rear. As always, his ears caught every wisp of sound, his body sensed every vibration in the earth, and as he breathed, every scent. All this he catalogued, creating a continuous image of his environment, keeping him always alert to changes that threatened danger.

He thought back to sniper school, the insistence of his asshole instructors to observe such discipline. At times, they tested the students and one or two were thrown out because they missed the signs of an approaching instructor posing as the enemy. "You are a risk to yourself, your spotter, and the Army!" the major in charge had screamed.

Even worse than ignoring the environment was to let the mind wander, and worst of all was to fall asleep. He'd done that only once, while on a three-day mission in Afghanistan. He'd awoken to see a Taliban tribesman downhill, sneaking upward, unaware he was on a collision course with his position. But snipers knew how to slice throats as well as how to pull triggers.

His attention snapped back to present time, on the island, on his mission.

Two hours later, when most of the houses had doused their lights behind closed shutters, a lone figure strode down the road through town.

His pulse quickened as he centered the man in his night-vision goggles. He focused on the shadowed face and felt his pulse quicken.

"Good God," he whispered.

It was Richard Drake. He displayed the same don't-mess-with-me manner, the strong jaw, as when they were in Afghanistan. He was a poster boy for Marine Recon. Drake turned off the road and traced a path upward, stopped at a cottage, and let himself in. No key. That was good to know.

The door shut and dim light shone through the jalousies. Twenty minutes later, the light went out. *He's gone to bed.*

CHAPTER 13

Richard arose at sunrise, ate a quick breakfast, and donned his usual gear, including his Marine-issue Ka-Bar sheath knife, Glock 17 pistol, canteen, grub, sat phone, and odds and ends..

He hiked eastward through the shadowed bush, above and east of town. *Just a walk in the park* was how he thought of his foray to the rainforest. Around him, morning birds gossiped and nighttime critters settled in for sleep.

The Coxon place lay a couple hundred yards up the mountain to his left. The morning breeze did not extend to the forest floor, but the night-time cool lingered and Richard hadn't broken a sweat in spite of his quick pace.

His plan was to descend to the valley floor by way of the same entrance Sophie used, located on the western side, about halfway along the length of the valley. He'd look for brooks, landmark outcroppings of rocks, and distinctive old-growth trees like those George had mentioned. These would serve as navigation landmarks. Also, he'd –

Richard stopped cold.

There was rustling in the woods to his right. A wandering Coxon dog?

Maybe. But it sounded more like the size of a deer, and it was coming closer. He faced the sound, but performed a quick three-sixty scan in case it was a distraction. Could it be the stranger, prowling the island? Or, worse, did the man have a partner?

The approaching sounds continued – cracking twigs and plainly audible footfalls. He stared through gaps between a thick growth of dry bushes. The intruder's sounds shifted to the right of the bushes, where the underbrush thinned, offering a clear line of sight.

Hmm. A spot of color, and movement, steady, and not particularly furtive. A person, his breath coming quickly, as if having grown fatigued from hiking up the mountain. There was something familiar about that breathing. And the footsteps.

Damn!

"Hi, Richard. You arrived early. I had to run to catch up. I almost missed you."

"What the bloody *hell* are you doing here?"

Sophie, face damp with sweat, closed the distance and disarmed him with a big, long kiss on his lips. At length, she broke off, and smiled into his eyes. "Surprised, huh?"

He tried unsuccessfully to scowl. "How did you know I'd be here, and not at another entrance to the valley?"

"I followed you from your bungalow. I had to, because I didn't know if you'd take this route or the one further north." She grinned. "When you turned off the road and entered the bush before reaching the track to the Coxons', I knew you'd take this entrance. If you'd continued on the road to the North Side, you'd be aiming for the northern entrance."

He forced a serious tone to his voice. "I suppose you think you're pretty smart, all suited up in jungle gear."

"Yup," she said, pointing out the high points of her outfit. "Long sleeves, hunting knife, boots, hair pulled under my rain-proof hat."

"Damn it, Sophie, this is dangerous."

"Well, I'm pretty dangerous myself."

She sidled close enough for him to smell soap and – *what?* "You wore perfume?"

"Just for this part. I had to neutralize you."

"Neutralize? What kind of a word is that?" He took a quick breath. Wondered how in hell she could captivate him at the same time he was really, really not liking that she wanted to go along.

"Neutralize?" she said, her eyes innocent. "It's one of those Marine words you use when you're telling George and Michael a war story. It's what you do to the enemy to make him stop shooting at you. Or, you know, scolding you."

"Sophie?"

"Yes," she whispered, and planted another big kiss on his tight lips, cutting off his next planned words.

Which he forgot. He slanted his eyes in wariness. *What a crafty, crafty minx.*

He shrugged. Wrapped his arms around her jungle-outfitted shoulders, and kissed her back.

After a minute, he pulled away and looked her in the eye. For some reason, a phrase came to mind – *the condemned man's final meal.*

He maintained a serious expression, neither angry nor, heaven forbid, completely accepting. "Okay. Here we go. First, nice outfit. It actually looks practical."

"Thank you. It's from an outfitter." She gestured. "And I have this official-looking daypack with other things, like food."

"Right. Second, I fully realize your tactics to get under my radar, and you succeeded. You may come with me."

"Oh," she said tentatively. "There's more, isn't there?"

"Yes. I know you're in great physical shape. You've been exploring the island, you run, and I wouldn't be surprised if you work out with weights. Also, you've got a green belt in karate, and you're very cool under pressure."

"Thanks," she said. "Is there a 'but' coming next?"

"There is. What will *probably* happen in the valley is a pleasant walk. But what *might* happen is that we meet the guy who attacked you, and he may even have friends. If he guy saw you as a threat before, worthy of killing, then he won't be any friendlier this time."

She swallowed. "Okay."

"We have to remain alert. We cannot talk. We cannot do anything that will indicate we are there. Also, we cannot leave signs that we have been there – like breaking a branch on a bush as we walk.

"Finally, I'll take the lead because that will give me the first look at the situation, and if we do run into this guy, I'll see him first. You stay about six feet behind. If the path gets too twisty and you can't see me, then get closer. If you want to get my attention, touch my shoulder."

She had let her jaw drop during the final few sentences. Her eyes were wide as saucers. "Um, okay."

"Can you remember all that?"

"May I ask a question?"

"Yes."

"Are you now my drill sergeant and I'm in Marine Force Recon or something?"

He stared hard at her, looking for a twitch at the corner of her lips or batted eyelashes.

She looked him in the eye and said, "That man attacked me and tried to stab me. I need to respond. I understand what I must do when we're in the valley and I promise to do exactly as you say."

Richard held out his hand and they shook.

He took the lead along the deer track, glanced back, checked her distance behind him – six feet, give or take – and continued onward. He felt like he was taking a competent new guy on his first patrol – able and willing to obey and to learn but completely naïve in the ways of war. He knew he must be on the lookout for both of their sakes.

At the valley rim, Richard paused and peered down at this new world, the lush greenery below, the leafy canopy and its random openings, some revealing tree branches, others showing grassy glades, and several making visible a ribbon of water flowing from north to south.

A breeze passed along the canopy, making it undulate like a giant green fabric. He found himself mesmerized, and at length let out his breath. He sensed Sophie, her hand on his shoulder, her breath warm upon his neck.

He reached for Sophie's hand and gave her a squeeze, maintained voice silence, and stepped forward on the track, which descended the valley wall at a steep angle. When they were beneath the canopy, the path turned muddy. He slowed and figured that was a good move anyway, enabling him to better listen and observe.

Flocks of parrots and parakeets raced among the trees, making a great racket. Insect chatter filled the cool, damp air. In the near distance, a deer stared at them, then loped away.

Richard was particularly struck by the foliage, which he surveyed with a military eye. An ambusher could hide behind trees, bushes, leaves, thick vines, and up in trees. He had to remind himself that even modest rock outcroppings in

Afghanistan provided cover as well. But here, possibilities for concealment and ambush appeared countless.

Then, he noticed variations. Under and near the trees, undergrowth was sparse, apparently because the wide, leafy branches decreased sunlight. Elsewhere, there was a mix of medium-size trees and undergrowth of lush plants, often with bright flowers in red and yellow and orange.

He surveyed the track they trod, looking for spots where mud showed on leaves, checking for evidence of passing deer or other critters, and for the presence of human boot prints. He found all except the boot prints.

After twenty minutes, having traveled north along the track bisecting the valley, he raised his hand and they stopped. Sophie remained six feet behind. Even better, she turned and faced their back trail, forming their rear guard. He scanned ahead and to the side, visually and with his ears.

The valley sounds and sights remained as they had been, a constant undertone of insects, punctuated by bird calls and flapping wings, the plop of water from leaves, the gentle breeze overhead.

He continued, looking for a place to rest, and chose a grassy glade off the track, near the babbling creek. Sophie joined him and they broke open snacks and drinks that they had each packed.

Richard opened the plastic wrapping of a First Strike Ration, light-weight, compact, and fairly edible, more so if you waited to eat it and got really hungry. He had selected a Beef Snack, BBQ, complemented by water from his canteen.

Sophie munched on a veritable picnic of deviled eggs, cut carrots, a few chips, and an apple, all washed down with great-smelling coffee that she shared. She glanced at his food and motioned that she'd share more than just coffee, but he shook his head. Right now, he needed nutrition and the calories provided by a First Strike Bar, affectionately called a 'Hooah! Bar.' They ate in companionable silence.

Richard's growing sense of familiarity with his new surroundings quickly gave way to Force Recon habits. He made a mental note to depart from the deer track as soon as they completed their initial circuit of the valley. Two reasons came to mind. One was security. If they left the track, their route became unknown to an enemy observer.

The other was opportunity. If they were free of the track, they could more easily explore possible sites where the stranger might locate his base camp and places where he could observe and ambush them.

He also thought of a third reason. Departing from the deer track vastly reduced the stranger's opportunities for learning of their passage by his setting of 'tells' – he could easily place tells on the well-travelled trails, but couldn't possibly cover the whole forest.

Richard chewed and swallowed quickly, anxious to continue.

CHAPTER 14

Sophie saw that Richard was finishing off what looked like a large candy bar. He was making getting-ready-to-go motions, packing all the wrappers and even smoothing the ground. She touched his shoulder and looked him in the eye. He paused.

She leaned close and whispered, "I need to talk."

"Okay, if we're quiet."

For some reason, she felt like they were on sort of a sleepover, where the lights were out but there was still stuff to say.

She banished the thought with a shiver. *This is much more dangerous than getting caught by an attentive mom.* She whispered, "What sort of things are you looking for?"

He chewed and swallowed the last of the candy bar and placed his lips close to her ear. "I needed to gauge what is 'normal' – the look and feel of the bushes, the sounds and the silences of the animals.

"It's all about becoming familiar with how things appear when no one has disturbed them. I've finished that part, and now I'm looking for places where the stranger might make his camp, and also places where he could hide."

"Hide?"

"Yes, to observe us and take our measure, or ambush us."

"Oh. What's a 'tell'?"

"Something an enemy puts in your way that he hopes you will disturb when you pass, informing him you were there."

"Like a branch in the middle of your path?"

"Yeah, that you could step on or brush aside."

"Have you seen any?"

"No."

"I'll look, too."

"Good. Are you ready to go?"

"Not yet, okay?"

"Okay."

She sensed he didn't want to remain in one place too long. He probably figured it gave the enemy time to find them and plan an ambush. She glanced around, like he was doing, checking that all was normal. She saw no lurking strangers.

She wasn't confident about identifying tells, which seemed like they could be pretty sneaky. But she vowed to look for them.

She gulped and thought, *My gosh! I' thinking like a Force Recon Marine!*

"I'll be quick," she said.

He nodded, and she gobbled the rest of her lunch, remaining so close to him she smelled the chocolate from his candy bar.

She also smelled his special scent, and immediately vanquished all the thoughts swirling around *that* discovery. She focused and asked, "What would his camp look like?"

"To begin with, it depends on the needs and the background of the stranger."

"Like whether or not he's trying to hide from the law?"

"Right. In that case, he'll search for a place that's high, that'll enable him to spot people down on the valley floor who are searching for him."

"Okay."

"Then, his choice will depend on his experience. A person new to the jungle will do one thing, maybe choose a tree and build a sleeping platform on a sturdy branch. A person more experienced in the woods might look for a ledge up the side of the valley with a drop-off on all sides, for easy defense. The experienced person would also look for a place with at least two escape routes."

"Which the tree guy wouldn't have," she said.

"Yup – there's only one way up or down the tree." He looked at her and tilted his head. "I didn't know you were interested in these things."

Sophie realized this was her opportunity to share with Richard her fear of being stalked again by a man like her ex-boyfriend, intent on killing her. She had shared this darkest fear with no one, not even Maren.

She had almost told Richard several times, but the timing hadn't seemed appropriate. She felt close to him and she loved him. But she also wanted to solve this problem on her own. Her solution was to find a place to hide on the island and stock it with several days' supplies. She had ordered the outfitter gear as part of her plan, having found that running shorts and even jeans left something to be desired when combing the woods.

She had yet to find a suitable hide, partly because she didn't know exactly what to look for. But the point was, she was helping herself, not depending on others. That part felt good. Her present turmoil came not because she had yet to find her hideaway, but whether to share her problem and her solution.

As she pondered, she didn't feel the fear that motivated her quest, but felt another emotion, a pang from holding back from telling Richard. Their bond strengthened daily, and to not share felt untrusting, unworthy of where they were in their intimacy.

She imagined that Maren would share her deepest fears with George, but they were married. Sophie wondered how a person better than herself, unmarried but in a close relationship, would feel at this moment. Perhaps she would feel shame, maybe even that her hideaway idea was correct but that Richard would lack the capacity to understand.

No, that's not right, she thought. She had no reason to be ashamed. She had been chased by one mad man, and brutally attacked by another. And as far as her fear and her plan, Richard would understand. She concluded that her present confusion was centered on whether she was ready to take her next step of intimacy with the man she loved. She smiled briefly and decided, *Yes, I'll take the step*. Decision made, she bent to one side and very deliberately set one twig on top of another in a particular way.

Then she told him, and he listened, eyes serious. He made sure she was finished, then said, "You know, I'm always here for you. George is, too. In fact, the whole population of St. Mark has your six."

She touched his cheek. "I know, and when I'm with you I feel perfectly safe. It's the only time I sleep through the night."

"But other times?"

"I feel vulnerable. I hope that if I find a place I know is safe from an attacker, I'll feel less vulnerable." She shrugged. "It's an idea. I want you to help me, but to start, I want to do the looking on my own. I think that will help."

He spoke quietly. "I like your idea. It makes sense. So, to begin, you want me to describe how to select a safe place, right?"

She nodded.

He rose and extended his hand, helped her to her feet. "Okay, let's go. I'll show you what you need to know. When you're ready, I can help you choose and fix up your place."

The remainder of the afternoon, they journeyed the length and breadth of the valley. Most of the time they were off the deer tracks, and Sophie found herself copying Richard's way of gently pushing branches aside, just enough to squeeze past, then moving them back to their normal position. Also, as he walked, he placed his feet to avoid twigs and branches, which she now realized could be tells.

He pointed out half a dozen places where the stranger might have decided to locate his camp. All were on steep sections of the valley wall, mostly on boulders or piles of rocks. They were still down at the level of trees and bushes, which gave cover for retreat or ambush. They were also compact. Richard said that if they discovered he'd chosen one of them it meant there was probably only one man, not a team.

As they crossed a deer track, Richard stopped and pointed at a short length of vine lying on the ground, supported at each end by a piece of branch. He gestured around at the foliage where they stood, then leaned close and whispered.

"Do you see any vines like that?"

Curious at the question, she examined their surroundings. "No. No vines."

He smiled and nodded at the length of vine on the ground. "Is that a tell, Sophie?"

She put her hand to her mouth. "Oh! Yes."

He continued, and she followed, careful not to disturb the tell. She shivered, thoroughly creeped out by the knowledge that the stranger had laid a trap for them.

CHAPTER 15

He scowled at what he saw from his place of concealment in the rainforest, frustrated at having to put up again with the girl, and now Richard Drake, tromping through his valley.

Drake moved like a combat vet, though he didn't seem fully at home in the close quarters of the rainforest. Sure, because Drake was accustomed to the wide-open spaces of Afghanistan. This must be his first rainforest experience. Good, that was an edge, but one the Marine would quickly overcome. A reason to move quickly to get what was his, then kill Drake and the girl.

He ran his hands through the irregular strands of burlap and jute streaming from his ghillie suit. It was hot and weighed a heavy nine pounds, but his desert-camo version back in the Army had saved him more than once. An enemy can't kill what they can't see.

He had ordered jungle-appropriate fabric shades for the present garment, and when he remained still, he blended perfectly with the rainforest. When he lay prone on the ground, a person would have trip over him to realize he was more than a hump of grass.

At length, the two interlopers departed through the girl's usual south exit on the west side. He was wary of Drake doubling back and waited thirty minutes before conducting a final visual scan.

Satisfied he was indeed along again, he hiked toward his base camp, drifting like an apparition, careful not to snag the ghillie suit strands on branches. As always, he selected a different route through the bush and avoided the deer tracks altogether. His tactics ensured him a margin of safety and of surprise, especially if one of the island locals wandered into the valley.

He used the gentle contours of the valley, rocks, and a dense stand of trees as landmarks to make his way back to his lair. After he stowed his gear and rations, he pulled off the ghillie suit and hung it on a branch to air out. He guzzled water.

As before, every several minutes he peeked through gaps in the foliage, gaining sight of the near perimeter, out to about fifty or seventy-five yards, depending on the direction, and then through other gaps to further reaches of the valley. He listened as well, his ears fully attuned to animal sounds – and to those times when the critters went silent.

The mid-day light was excellent, which meant he had time to check tells and to provide a surprise for intruders. He grabbed a daypack, loaded tools he'd need and descended to the valley floor.

Through a circuitous route, he walked to where he originally sighted the girl. He moved off the track and found a glade bordered by thick bushes. It was a perfect place for an intruder to stop and rest.

He checked the two narrow entrances to the glade. What he wanted was a pair of two mature trees, one on either side of the entrance. These he found and recalled that he had waited behind one when stalking the girl.

A magnificent tree dominated the center of the glen. One limb had been sawn off, and two sections of it lay on the ground. They were obviously the trimmed ends, each about a foot in diameter. Cut by who, he had no idea – some person who wanted wood for furniture, art, whatever. All he cared about was that he could use them for a trap. Each section was two feet long and weighed about twenty pounds. Perfect for what he had in mind.

Within twenty minutes, he had rigged both sections, one to each of the trees. In repose, they hung down over the center of the entrance path at waist height, supported by parachute cord.

He swung them away from the path, one to the left, the other to the right, and secured them with slip knots to branches about eight feet off the ground. He led the cord from the slip knots to a trip wire that he stretched across the path at ankle height.

Carefully, he stooped and pulled the trip cord. It didn't take much force – much less than that of a person walking. He heard nothing until the last split second. There was a whoosh and then the two sections collided with a resounding thump in the middle of the path.

He visualized the person who tripped his booby trap, chagrinned at almost falling, pausing to look down at the trip cord, and becoming a target for the twin battering rams that would appear out of nowhere and bash their hips. The result would be two terrible bruises at the very least. More likely, there would be other damage as well, possibly a broken bone and torn ligaments.

Whoever bore the brunt of the trap, he did not care. Whether it was the girl, or Drake, his own plan was enhanced. Terror was delivered. Uncertainty established. He would have raised the stakes. The island would continue focus on exactly what he dictated – a dangerous stranger in their midst who targeted the girl.

He cocked the trap and retied the slip knots, then gently covered the trip cord with leaves. He stepped back and nodded in approval. The trip wire was concealed on the ground, and in the trees, limbs and leaves hid the supporting cords.

Next, he checked the three tells he had set in other parts of the valley. One to the south was tripped. Judging by boot marks on nearby ground, Drake or the girl had tripped it. The other two remained untouched.

He squatted at the untouched tells. He searched for evidence of a person passing by and found more boot marks. *Damn.* They were here and avoided the tells. That was no accident and was bad news – his quarry was already too attuned to the rainforest.

He set three fresh tells at random, two on tracks and one in the gap between two thorn bushes, a natural route for a person who was traveling off the deer tracks.

Viewing the image of the muscular Marine in his mind's eye, his chest tightened. Drake would not back off. He felt himself smiling as he remembered the gorge and the rapids. He deftly unsheathed his Afghan fighting knife, what they called a *peshkabz,* and tested the razor edge, the needle point, and nodded in satisfaction.

CHAPTER 16

The morning began well enough for Sophie and indeed everyone on the island. Uncle John returned from St. Thomas on the ferry, walking and smiling.

It seemed that the whole island greeted him at the pier, each person sharing a bit of news and wishing him good health. After forty-five minutes, Sophie intervened.

"He needs rest," she told the woman talking to Uncle John. "He's been through a lot of tests and a long trip home on a rolling ferry."

"Oh my," the woman said, patting Uncle John on the shoulder. "Yes, by all means. Get some rest. We'll see you soon. Welcome home, dear man."

He smiled at his friends, and they waved him on his way.

Sophie ushered him along the street and into the store, observed his pronounced stoop and labored breathing, and declared, "You need to rest. Let's get you to bed."

"I'm afraid you're right, Sophie."

Which chilled her. The man never took her suggestion to rest.

"I just need a little shut-eye," he murmured, stretching out on his bed. "How's the store? Any problems?"

"Everything is fine, no problems." She'd tell him about the stranger another time. Now he needed rest.

"Oh," he responded absently.

She pulled off his shoes and draped his light blanket over him. He didn't seem to notice.

He folded his hands over his chest. Grimaced.

Sophie frowned. "Was that chest pain?"

"Yeah. Could you hand me my pills, Sophie?"

She rummaged in a paper bag he had carried, dumped out two prescription cards and two bottles of white pills. "Which ones?"

"The little ones. They're for the twinges I get."

Sophie got him a glass of water and gave him the pills. He swallowed and lay back. His face was pale and his voice sounded as if he'd aged a decade during his days in St. Thomas.

An awful thought hit her, and she asked gently, "Uncle John, what did the doctors say? Did they think it was time for you to leave the hospital?"

His voice was reedy. "I had to be firm with the doctors. You know how they are. Always another test. Another day hanging around looking at the ceiling."

So, the man took off with bare approval, if that. And a worse thought occurred. *Uncle John has come home to die.*

She gulped and turned from him to hide the tears streaming down her face. "I'll leave you to rest, but I'll be in the store. Call if you need anything." At the door, she glanced back at him. His eyes were shut. Features gaunt. He slept.

In the store, behind the counter, Sophie didn't bother to stifle her tears. She covered her face with her hands and cried for the kind man who had taken her in, given her work, and treated her like a beloved daughter. Oh God. Please.

Sophie rummaged around for a tissue and dabbed her tears. She felt adrift, as though she were about to lose a father, one of those people who is not supposed to die.

She questioned that feeling. Her own situation seemed so insignificant compared with the terrible grief she also felt. Was 'feeling adrift' okay? Or was she being overly possessive of Uncle John? After all, he was his own person, not hers.

Heck, he seemed resigned and even comfortable to pass from this life. Who was she to wish him to stay? Why shouldn't she simply allow him to accept the gravity of his illness and leave in peace?

Maybe she should talk with him, comfort him, give him support in his decision of acceptance. That seemed the right thing to do, instead of moping about like a spoiled child.

She scanned the counter as if seeing it for the first time. It had always served as a place to set groceries and supplies when checking out. Now she viewed the scarred wooden surface as something extra. Not pretty, but built for utility, a link in a business transaction. Also, it was a place to lean on and to weep.

Hours later, after all the shoppers had come and gone, she heard Uncle John stir. She heated soup for him, which he enjoyed. He insisted she keep to her normal routine and return to her cottage at the Coxons' and to relay his best wishes to the family.

Reluctantly, she agreed. "I'll be here tomorrow morning."

"Okay. I'll be fine." He smiled. "I'm happy to be back and it's great to see you, Sophie. You are the light of my life. Oh, along with Jenny and her gang."

"The lollipop thieves?"

"Yes, bless their black hearts." He chuckled and, for a moment, he was the old Uncle John.

She reached down and took his hand. "Uncle John, I love you. You've been like a father and a treasured friend to me. You accepted me and let me work with you."

He blinked and looked up at her. "You are the treasure, Sophie. You gave an old man sunshine in his – well, his days here on the island. I know where I am in life, and I'm comfortable."

He gave her a hand a squeeze, and she felt an abiding understanding pass between them. They remained silent, and then he shut his eyes and drifted into sleep. She closed the door quietly, still feeling adrift.

Sophie waited in front of the store for George and Michael, on their way home from the boatyard, and the three of them trudged up the hill and through the shaded track to home. Sophie freshened up in her cottage and joined the family for dinner at the big table in the main house. She shared her concern with Uncle John's health and they agreed that his condition was serious.

"I'm glad you're there," Maren said, "making sure he gets rest and takes his pills. Also, we need to remember that it's his first day back, and the ferry trip was a strain for sure. Let's hope he'll be better tomorrow morning."

The others nodded gravely. Jenny wiped away a tear. Sophie changed the subject to exploring the valley with Richard.

"I can't believe he let you go with him," Maren said.

Sophie made a face. "I had to agree to follow right behind him, not talk, and obey all his orders."

George laughed.

Maren scowled.

Sophie said, "He was right. We found a tell, a piece of vine that the stranger wanted us to disturb as we passed, so he'd know we were there."

George frowned. "Hmm, leave it to Richard to think of looking for that sort of thing. I guess it means the intruder had military training."

"We never did see him. Richard pointed out places where he could be hiding."

"His camp?" George asked.

"Yes. Richard figured it would be high, like on the side of the valley, not in the center."

"Not in a circle of thorn bushes in the rainforest?" Maren mused. "It would be harder to get into, but he'd have several escape routes."

Sophie shrugged. "Could be. Richard did point out one place like that. No, come to think of it, that place was on the edge of the valley, on a rocky ledge up about fifteen feet. But it was surrounded by thick bushes."

"The others, they were on the edge of the valley?" George asked.

"Yes, mostly on rocks. Some covered with trees and bushes and vines. Others pretty bare. Anyone would have to lie low not to be seen."

"And stay back from the lip," George said. "It sounds like you got a good look at the valley. Richard said he wanted to familiarize himself with the place." He looked at Maren. "He said we were going to do more of the same tomorrow."

"He's going back?" Sophie asked.

George nodded. "He asked me to show him around, especially features that may serve as the guy's base camp, or where he could set a booby trap. Richard didn't mention tells. I guess they could be anywhere."

"Will you try to find the man?" Sophie asked.

"Not tomorrow," George said. "It sounded to me like Richard wanted to memorize the valley, to know all the details, to be prepared. He said we would avoid contact, and if we saw the guy, we'd   back   off."

CHAPTER 17

Richard followed George into the valley, this time through a different entrance, located further north, though still on the western side of the valley. The air was misty, and a drizzle pattered on the leaves as they descended the twisty track.

As before, he noticed the huge variation in the density of the rainforest foliage. One moment they were immersed in a thick grove of bushes and the next in a grassy glade.

At one of these glades, George gestured and whispered, "This is the king of the forest. The largest tree, hundreds of years old."

"You sound respectful, calling it a king." Richard gazed up the tall trunk, extending through the canopy.

George placed his hand on the rough, wet bark. "Yes, respect for living that long and for history, I guess. It's a big-leaf mahogany, lives to three-hundred-fifty years. It was a sapling about the time my pirate ancestor landed – John Coxon.."

"Makes sense to me," Richard said. "We Marines respect our history. We call it 'tradition' but it's the same idea."

"This is the one tree I will never cut. Others, I'll cut a limb when I need it for a boat. The tree itself survives just fine. Here, I'll show you."

They walked another ten minutes. Richard was now soaked from the continuing rain, its hiss drowning out the insects, leaving him with a creepy, closed-in feeling. For a moment, he wished for a dose of Afghan heat.

George pushed through a barrier of thick bushes and into another glade. Richard noticed a gap on the far side, but otherwise the glade was firmly walled in. George pointed to a tree with a forked trunk and a wide spread of leafy branches. "That's a West Indies mahogany. Only grows to seventy-five feet. A month back, I sawed off a branch from right there. The branch made a wonderful keel for a fishing boat."

He looked around the ground beneath where the branch had been cut. "Hmm, I trimmed off each end, but the pieces are gone. Too bad – I wanted you to see the grain."

Richard had a funny feeling in his stomach. "Are you sure you didn't take those pieces, or throw them into the bushes?"

"Positive." He smiled. "No problem. Come on, we can continue around the valley. We're looking for places where the stranger could make a base camp, right?" He strode toward the other gap in the bushes.

"No!" Richard said sharply. "Don't move."

He approached the other gap, lowered himself to hands and knees, and carefully brushed away leaves. A thin cord, ankle high, stretched across the path through the gap.

He looked up at the trees on either side. All appeared normal. He stood and pushed a limb aside, revealing a continuation of the trip cord. It led to a short length of tree limb, where it was tied off in a slip knot. Another line supported the limb, so that when the slip knot was pulled, the limb was released to swing in an arc, down and into the space above the path, and crash into whoever tripped the slip knot. The same set-up was arranged on the other side of the path.

Richard approached George and whispered. "It's a booby trap. Stay here and watch."

Richard found a long, forked stick and pushed the forked end at the trip cord, the same way a person's foot would push if striding by.

He looked up just in time to see the released lengths of limb swing down toward each other. With a loud crack, they collided exactly in the center of the gap.

George's face turned a sickly green.

Richard dropped the forked stick and muttered, "I guess we know what that could do someone passing by."

"I guess," George said tightly. "Hell, that could smash a man's bones – cripple him for life."

Richard patted his holstered Glock 17. "This guy's playing for keeps. But so are we."

"What the hell is his motive?"

Richard shook his head. "Sophie and I have been over it a hundred times. We don't have a clue why this guy is after her, or whether she was in the wrong place at the wrong time. He might be connected to Sophie's violent ex-boyfriend, but that seems like a long shot. Then again, maybe he's on the run from the law."

"What now, Richard?"

"I'd like to show you a possible camp. See what you think. Then we'll leave."

"As long as we don't run into the bastard. I'll murder him. Screw the law."

"I believe you would," Richard said. "Bare-handed. But you're okay to check out this one place? Then we're out of here. Enough for one day."

"Just show me where."

"It's further south on the west side. Easy to spot."

"Big rock on the rim wall?"

"That's the one."

"A natural," George said. "I took the kids camping there once, right after we saw 'Jurassic Park' during a visit to St. Thomas. They kept asking if the raptors could reach the top of the rock where we slept. I said we'd be safe."

"Did the dogs come along?"

"Is the Pope Catholic?"

"Were they nervous?"

"Good point. No, the dogs knew the biggest animal on the island was a four-point buck. They slept curled up in a pack. Would you like me to show you a good route to get there? It's not a deer track, but it passes through old growth pretty much free of sticker bushes."

"Lead on."

They walked in silence for half an hour, then veered to the right. The valley wall came into view through breaks in the foliage. George quietly moved next to a thick tree, its trunk blocking him from anyone on the black boulder. Richard drew close.

George whispered, "Is that the one you were thinking of?"

"Yeah. It hit me as logical. There's a good view from up there, steep sides to prevent someone from climbing up and surprising you, and probably a couple of ways out."

"All of that and more. Come on."

George approached the joint between boulder and valley rim and pointed. "These form steps. It's the only way up."

"Okay. Let me take the lead, just in case."

Richard positioned himself at the base of the rocky ladder and began the climb, testing the rocks for stability. Near the top, he cautiously raised his head over the lip. He scanned the flat surface and released his breath, relieved to find no one there.

He quickly ascended and rolled onto the top of the rock and, just to be safe, lay silent for two minutes, hearing only the usual insect and bird sounds.

He stood and walked to the ladder. "It's clear. Come on up."

George ascended, brushed off his hands, and looked around. "Yep, there's what's left of our fire."

Richard glanced at the ashes, knelt and prodded with his finger. "Soaking wet." As he stood, he noticed an depression in the wall. "Is that a cave?"

George nodded. "The kids were convinced that was where the raptors lived. Till the dogs sniffed around inside and returned with wagging tails."

"Did you explore it?"

"Yeah. I guess you've seen Jenny and her gang at the blow hole west of town?"

"Below the precipice?"

"Yes. Well, she's fascinated with caves. On our island, we hear stories of buried pirate treasure. The kids embellish those and have almost convinced themselves there's gold and jewels in behind the blow hole. Luckily, they have the sense not to go in there, with the waves rolling in and spewing out the top. Anyway, we explored this cave, just to be sure there was no treasure back there."

Richard reached into his daypack.

George chuckled. "Damn, you must've been a great Boy Scout. You have a flashlight in there?"

"Yes." Richard pulled it out and headed into the cave.

George followed, pulling out his own flashlight. Like Richard's, it was small, made of tough metal, and its light was very bright. When Richard glanced at it and smirked, George chuckled. "Yeah, me too, I guess. We didn't find any deep holes in the floor, but the walls and ceiling do close in, so watch those. The rock is pretty uneven."

Richard shined his flashlight into the many nooks and crannies on either side, taking his time. Around a bend, the cave narrowed, forcing him to lean down and scoot sideways.

"There," he said, pointing the light at an object stuffed toward the back of a fissure.

"Not ours. We took everything with us."

Richard reached back and touched fabric. He poked it and felt cans inside. "Feels like it's soup cans."

"Shall we pull it out?"

"Not yet. Let's keep looking. See how big the total stash is. I've got a couple ideas."

"Which include poison, I hope."

"Maybe."

Continuing into the cave, Richard found two more stashes and George found one in a rock pocket in the overhead.

"The tunnel's really narrowing down," Richard said.

He glanced toward where the entrance lay, about a hundred feet back, past three twists. He'd allowed ten minutes to explore, figuring beyond that they'd risk the stranger either happening by or coming by design, having tracked them. They were now at nine-and-a-half minutes.

George must have read his thoughts. "About ready to get out?"

"Yeah. But one question – how far back can you go?"

"I don't know. This is about as far as the kids and I got, but the dogs went further. These kinds of tunnels can go on for a long time, or they can peter out. Just depends on mother nature."

"Okay, I'm set."

George turned and led the way out of the winding cave. Outside, the rain was still falling, and mist hung in the valley – all very creepy as far as Richard was concerned.

Richard walked to the ladder of rocks and checked that it was empty. He surveyed what he could see of the surrounding forest and moved close to George. "I'm ready to get out of this place."

"Amen to that. What shall we do with all the stuff in the cave?"

"I'm thinking this is the stranger's backup camp. Knowing that gives us an edge. But only if we don't touch his stuff and tip him off."

"Yeah. If we chase him out of his base camp, it'll be a good guess that he's run to this place."

"Right. Depending on how threatened he feels, he may want to hide here for a few days. One other thing," Richard added quietly.

"Sure."

"I'm still wondering if that cave has another entrance. What's your best guess?"

George's eyes lit up with cruel mischief.

Richard blinked in surprise. *The man must have the soul of a pirate.*

"What?" George asked.

"Has anyone ever told you that your ancestor's blood runs in your veins?"

"Maren, sometimes."

Richard shook his head in mock horror. "Okay, what do you think about another entrance to the cave?"

"Could be. Like I said, they can wander around for quite a distance."

"Where do you think it could come out?"

George gazed at the valley wall, then up at the rim. "My wild guess is it would tend to rise. Yeah, continue back into the ground and rise. You may find it, looking like a small sink hole, close to the rim. Did you notice a little breeze when we were inside?"

"No."

"Well, I did. That means there's another opening."

"Big enough for a man?"

"Wow, there's a thought. But there's no way of telling without finding it."

Richard turned toward the ladder. He had the answer he was seeking. It could be of use downstream, or not. The other entrance might be tiny or quite wide. Visible or covered in grass and leaves. He shrugged and began his descent.

As he waited at the bottom for George, he sensed someone watching him. He casually scanned the woods. Saw only trees and bushes in the swirling mist.

Damn. If it was the man they were after, he'd managed to tail them, perhaps during their entire time in the valley. Not good. Plus, he knew that they'd discovered his backup camp. Now, he'd move his stuff and set up an alternate. Or maybe leave his stuff to make us think he hadn't seen us. And still set up an alternate.

This man must not be underestimated.

When George joined him, Richard whispered, "Do you get the funny feeling someone's looking at you?"

George shut his eyes for a moment then opened them. "Yeah, but it's subtle, at the edge of your mind, sneaky-like."

"Right. Me, too. How about those times when you were out here in the valley alone, cutting wood? Did you ever get the feeling then?"

George looked at him and obviously he got the point – because his eyes turned hard as flint.

"Not once."

CHAPTER 18

Sophie waited behind the counter as a late-afternoon customer wandered the aisles, making her selections.

"I got a late start," the woman said. "Now I need something for a quick-fix dinner."

"Did you sleep late?"

The woman laughed. "No, nothing as fun as that. I went with my youngest to the blow hole. She's not old enough to join Jenny and her gang."

"I guess they're all nine or ten years old."

"Yup. Big kids. My little one has heard all the stories of the waves, the water spout, and the adventure of being splashed."

"You took her?"

The woman nodded. "Jenny and her gang invited her out on a safe rock to experience the thrill for herself. We spent the whole morning. I brought a little picnic for everyone." She grinned at Sophie. "I guess it's canned soup for dinner." She set two cans of beef soup on the counter, and Sophie checked her out.

They said their good-byes. Sophie waited a while, then slipped back to Uncle John's room.

She was surprised to find him awake. "Hi, Uncle John. How're you doing?"

"Fine," he said in his weak voice.

He looked paler than ever. Sophie smiled at him. "May I get you anything?"

"No. I'll just wake up a little and join you. Is everything okay out front?"

"Oh sure. I'll be there, restocking from this morning."

She left him and continued through the store, feeling her heart rate skyrocket. *He's in no shape to get out of bed, much less help me in the store.* Outside, her latest customer was talking with a friend under the big shade tree. Sophie approached the two women. "I have a favor to ask."

"Sure," they said in unison, no doubt reading the worry in her eyes.

"Uncle John looks even weaker than last night when he came home from the hospital. And his voice is no more than a whisper. I think it's time for Jimmy to take a look."

"Jimmy Franklin's a medic, Sophie," the customer said gently. "He's not a doctor."

"Yes," Sophie said, "but he can tell us if Uncle John needs to go to the hospital. Maybe I'm worrying over nothing. It would be reassuring, at the least."

The two women nodded. "I'll get him," the customer said.

Sophie touched her shoulder. "Tell him to hurry. Please."

She returned to the store, absently restocked cereal, soup, and condensed milk. After a few minutes she heard approaching footsteps.

Jimmy entered with his Army-issue canvas medical satchel slung over his shoulder.

"Hi, Doc," Sophie said. "Thanks for coming."

"Sure. Is he in back?"

"Yes. He hasn't gotten out of bed all day." She led the way and waited with folded arms as Jimmy checked the old man's pulse and blood pressure then put a gizmo on his finger to measure blood oxygen.

Jimmy replaced his instruments and picked up two plastic pill bottles from Uncle John's bedside table. He read the labels.

"You're taking both of these?" he asked.

Uncle John nodded. "One every six hours, the other in case I get pain in my chest or arm."

"Hmm," Jimmy said. "You didn't have a heart attack, right?"

"No heart attack, but there's problems. It's all a mystery to me, but I take the pills."

"When was the last time you took this pill for pain?"

"A couple of hours ago."

"Did it help?"

"Um. Well. Not really."

"Uncle John, you know pain is a signal of danger from your heart. We have to listen, okay? Do you have pain now?"

"Nothing I can't deal with."

Jimmy put a calm hand on Uncle John's shoulder. "We need to get you back to St. Thomas."

Uncle John turned his head toward the wall. Jimmy stared at the man in silence then looked at Sophie and shrugged. What could they do?

She blinked away a tear.

When Uncle John turned back, he looked up at Jimmy, without a single worry wrinkle in his face. "Doc, I hear you. Could I talk with Sophie for a couple of minutes?"

"Sure." Jimmy took a step toward the door and paused. "Shall I call for a helo? We could get you into the hospital in an hour. They can help you there."

"No need, Doc."

Jimmy departed quietly. Sophie heard his steps as he moved into the store, where they paused. *He's waiting for me.*

She looked at Uncle John. "You should go. You know that, don't you?"

He shook his head a fraction. "I came to this island twenty years ago. My leg wasn't wounded in an accident like people think, at least not the usual kind. It was in combat. I was a sergeant in the Army." He gave her his special smile. "That's why this room and the store are neat. Old habits." He went silent for a minute, as if coming to a decision.

"Sophie, you're like the daughter I never had. I never got the chance to get married and start a family. When I graduated from high school, back home in Baltimore, I worked the docks, loading and unloading ships. I had to join the union of course, which was as crooked as a witch's finger.

"I discovered one of the union bosses stealing from cargo boxes we'd just unloaded, not just dribs and drabs, but what we all knew was valuable artwork. I reported him, but the police were in on the deal and leaked word to the union. Read – the mob."

"Oh, my," she breathed.

"There were no charges brought against the union boss, but I was a marked man. I knew it was only days before I'd have a crippling or even fatal accident. So, I joined the Army. I never looked back."

He gazed at the ceiling, his chest heaving. *The emotion*, thought Sophie. *And his heart.*

He looked her in the eye. "This island is my home. The folks here are all the family a man ever needed."

"Uncle John," she whispered. "I can go with you on the helo to St. Thomas. I can stay with you in the hospital. They'll bring a cot into your room so I can sleep there and keep you company."

He blinked. "This is my home, Sophie." He reached out and took her hand.

CHAPTER 19

Night lingered, the sky black, stars bright. Cicadas and crickets jabbered. He had lain in at his usual spot above the tiny town for three hours. Figuring everyone was asleep, he rose and shouldered his daypack.

Stepping carefully, moving down and along the steep grade, he felt his way to the clearing at the front of the store. He stood for a minute behind the big tree, listening and watching. All was clear.

He crossed the clearing, opened the front door, and eased inside, shining his penlight at shelves burdened with food and supplies. The red lens made everything look mysterious, as if a stronger light would reveal secrets. He knew that wasn't the case, but that was the feeling he had. It always made him a little jumpy.

He remembered the traps they'd set back in Afghanistan for snipers like him. The enemy there was smart, not in a book way, but in the way of war.

They had all been young and full of themselves, us and them. But he had some book learning, at least the Army version. He knew their tricks. Back then, stuff that looked innocent did have secrets. *Sure as hell*, he thought. Move a rock out of your way and you might have just pulled the pin of a grenade. Bam, you're dead meat.

The sound of snoring drifted from the back room, then a cough. The rattle of pills. More coughing. Sounded painful. So, the old fart was sick.

He remembered the look on the girl's face the previous night. He'd thought she was worked up about her brush with death in the valley, but now he decided she was concerned about the old guy. Someone called him Uncle John.

He decided to give the man a visit. He crept to the back of the store and lifted the hinged access leaf on the countertop. Eased into the back room, smelled old-man sweat. *Damn,* he'd shut the windows tight, same as the other islanders. Scared of ghosts.

Like a shadow, he entered the back room. The old guy stirred.

"Sophie? Is that you?"

He froze where he stood, at the foot of the bed. Hoped the old geezer didn't have a flashlight. The guy coughed and for a moment he seemed to doze, but no, he asked again.

"Jimmy? I'm staying. I'm staying here."

Then the only sound in the room was the old man's labored breathing. He felt sorry for this Uncle John. The old guy stirred again.

"I love you, Sophie, like a daughter. You're the best."

His breathing was raspy, like the guys back in Afghanistan dying from a shot to the lung. Only the air didn't whistle through a hole in this guy's chest. Whatever. He probably wouldn't last the night.

The sniper remained another minute to be sure the old guy was fully asleep, then passed back into the store, shutting the door quietly behind him. He was angry at the old fool for being there and wondered at an unfamiliar sensation in his chest. He paused in the darkness, among cans of soup and boxes of cereal.

The unexpected pang was from his past, the sniper realized, a long-dormant memory somehow connected with the old guy, who was so close to death he couldn't draw a decent breath.

He was all about loving that girl – Sophie – like a daughter. Witnessing a dying man displaying such love had gotten under the sniper's skin.

He blinked and found himself back as a scrawny kid, when he still saw his dad was a god, to be obeyed without question. But Dad was a disciplinarian with a mile-wide soft streak for Mom and the kids. As a kid, the sniper had felt that love like a big lump in his heart, as real as a baseball.

His hand brushed against a shelf and a can fell to the floor, the sound pulling him back to the present, alert to the old guy awakening. He breathed silently and listened. Heard only the buzzing of insects outside and snoring from the next room.

The sniper couldn't believe he was this affected by ancient history. A father's love. All that was gone for him. He was in a different place now, on a mission. The point was, should he set the charge and likely harm or kill the old man? Or should he come back later, when no one was there?

The logical choice was to follow through with the mission. Hell, the old fart was going to die anyway, like a lung-shot soldier on the field of battle. You stopped the flow of blood, gave him morphine, and waited a few hours for him to die.

What would the instructors at sniper school say? *The mission comes first*. Okay, to hell with love. Carry out the mission. Set the charge.

No. The old man was worthy, not a piece of collateral damage. That made sense. Let the guy go in peace. Let the girl find his face calm, having gone to sleep and never awoken. He'd come back tomorrow. Tonight, he would honor the love.

Outside, a light blinked on in one of the houses. For some godforsaken reason, he recalled being awakened when his little brother had nightmares. He'd turn on the light and read the little guy a story and tuck him in. Yeah, even he had had a streak of love.

Back then, before the army and all that came after.

CHAPTER 20

The next morning, Sophie arrived at the store escorted by George and Michael. Just to be safe.

"Should we wait?" George asked.

"No, I'll be fine."

"You sure?"

She looked at the door, thinking of Uncle John asleep in his bed. Visualizing the store itself empty of a man lurking with his knife. *Or not.*

George seemed to sense her hesitation. "We'll wait five minutes. Give us a high sign."

"Okay," she said, surprised that she felt relief.

She opened the door, put the rock in place to hold it open in the breeze, entered, and began opening shutters. *Amazing how people took on the local customs,* she thought. Here was a man who was raised in Baltimore, for gosh sakes, yet he followed the local custom of insisting she close the shutters at night. He must have assumed she knew the reason was to keep the Jumbees out. *Oh well.*

Finding no intruders, and admonishing herself for ever thinking there was any danger, she hummed a calypso tune she'd heard from the locals. She walked the aisles and straightened a couple of cereal boxes. Everything was in order. She stuck her head out and waved at George and Michael.

"See you at lunch time," George said as he and Michael turned toward his boatyard.

Oh yeah, today is Saturday – the store and boatyard were open only half a day.

Sophie set her tote bag on the counter. She removed a plastic container with breakfast for John, including a cup of Maren's tea. A bird sang outside as she entered his room.

The air was curiously still. The bird had stopped singing. Cicadas hummed. Or was that her imagination? No, they were there. The wooden floor creaked as she leaned over to examine Uncle John's face in the morning shadow.

His eyes were closed, his expression serene.

But something was not right. He lay completely motionless, like a statue.

As if – Oh my God! Her hand flew to her mouth and she felt a chill.

Sophie leaned close and listened. Silence – no breathing.

She put two fingers to the side of his neck. There was no pulse.

John is dead, her mind told her. *You knew it would happen.* Well, it happened. Though still it seemed surreal.

After a final look at his inert form, with tears streaming down cheeks, she forced herself to walk from the room. There were things that had to done.

She continued along the aisle and out the door. Everything appeared as it had five minutes previously. Three dogs dozed under the tree. Up the mountain, a woman hung laundry. All looked normal. But things were not at all normal.

Uncle John was gone. She sobbed. Sophie needed people. For herself and for Uncle John.

There, past town, were George and Michael, almost at the boatyard. She sprinted half the distance and called out, not too loudly. She didn't want the whole population converging, asking questions, not just yet.

George and Michael turned, seemed to recognize her anguished expression, and rushed to her side.

George asked, "Is that man in the store?"

Sophie sobbed. "No, the stranger's not inside. But Uncle John – he's dead."

George gave her a hug and she hugged him back. They made their way to a building that now seemed very empty to Sophie. Inside the back room, George leaned over the bed and placed a callused hand under Uncle John's nose. A finger at his throat.

"You're right, Sophie. He's gone." He turned to Michael. "Son, go for Jimmy. Tell him Uncle John has passed. Ask him to come."

"Okay, Dad," Michael said, his voice choked.

Sophie gently pulled the light blanket over Uncle John's face.

George gave her a shoulder squeeze. "It was his time. Last night he said his good-bye to you."

She wiped her eyes. "I was hoping he'd agree to go to the hospital this morning."

"It's been coming," George said, blinking.

"He made his choice," she said, "didn't he?"

"He did. Independent, choosing his own way."

"His last words to me were 'This is my home, Sophie.' I guess that was his way of telling me."

Footsteps approached and Jimmy and Michael entered the room. Jimmy turned down the blanket, checked for breath and pulse, and nodded. He set the blanket back in place and let out a long breath. "I'll start the medical arrangements. A doctor will need to come over to the island to confirm cause of death."

"Will they take his body?" Sophie asked.

"No," Jimmy said. "We can bury him on the island. That's permitted."

"Or at sea." George said. "Many mornings I found him sitting on the pier watching the sea as the sun rose."

"In the evening, too," Michael said. "When we were returning home from work."

George nodded. "Yes. He'd be sitting on the pier. Waved to us as we passed, a smile on his face."

"I saw him, too, many mornings," murmured Sophie.

Jimmy asked, "You're thinking we bury him at sea?"

Everyone nodded.

"Okay," Jimmy said. "That's what I'll tell the coroner, or whoever comes over. Hmm, also we need to notify Uncle John's next of kin."

Sophie said, "He spoke to me about a brother. Maybe he has other brothers or sisters. They may want to take his remains for burial in a family plot. I'll look in Uncle John's room for phone numbers and make some calls."

George spoke quietly, as if organizing his thoughts, "I'll start the word going around. People will want to help. Maybe the fishermen can take charge of the burial at sea. We can all go out in boats to participate.

"There'll be a service, a gathering afterward. Michael, you tell folks at the boatyard. Some may want to leave to tell their wives, which is fine. I don't think we'll get a whole bunch of work done today, but that's okay." He glanced at the form in the bed. "It's our way of paying respects."

"I'll go and tell Maren," Sophie said, and then thought, *we can cry on each other's shoulder*.

Quietly, they departed. Sophie hiked up the road and turned right, onto the shady track to the Coxon home.

Lost in thought, she didn't pay attention to the trees and bushes or hear the birds and insects, but in her mind's eye relived good times with Uncle John.

His jokes with shoppers about which brands he should stock. Him pretending to be distracted, while letting the kids swipe an extra lollipop, and accepting their pennies in payment when they returned with guilty faces. The confidences he shared with Sophie about the island, its folks, and its stories.

About the halfway along the track, Sophie noticed that no birds fluttered through the upper branches, no insects chirped. She increased her pace, remembering another time when she got into trouble on this track.

The trees seemed to encroach, hemming her in. To either side, the woods appeared full of shadowed nooks where none had been a moment before.

She drew a calming breath. Paused mid-stride, shut her eyes, decided on a mini-meditation, aware of her surroundings yet keeping her mind clear.

On the count of five, she heard a bird in the distance.

On eight, insects resumed their chirping over to the right.

On nine she wondered why they didn't chirp on the left. She decided to move, anxious to be on her way, with or without a clear mind.

On ten, with one foot about to step forward, a deafening explosion tore the air. A tree whooshed past her, its branches sweeping down her face and body, and crashing across the track.

Sophie's eyes popped open. She saw a smoking stump to her left just off the path, and the fallen tree, quivering.

She stepped away from its grasping branches and wiped leaves from her clothing. A thought jumped into her head – *it's that man.*

She screamed into the underbrush, "You bastard! Who are you? What do you want?"

A dozen feet within the woods stood a fuzzy figure, indistinct in shadow and further undistinguishable because it was garbed in mottled green fluff, blending perfectly with the forest.

The figure turned toward her. A man's face was covered in splotches of green and brown. The stranger! Their eyes met for the briefest moment and then, smooth as a dancer, he drifted up the mountain. His feet appeared to float, his winding path avoided trees in a ghostly way, and as the distance increased, his fuzzy form faded until only the forest remained.

Sophie eyed the now-still tree lying across the track. Its weight would have crushed her dead. Had the stranger succeeded, he no doubt would now be standing over her, gloating.

She had survived again, but she knew he was not done with her. As she skirted the tree, she kept her movements slow, because her arms and legs shook so badly.

CHAPTER 21

Richard poked his head into Anika's office at The Danish Touch in downtown Charlotte Amalie, St. Thomas, where she worked as a manager and buyer.

"Hi, Anika."

She got up from behind her desk and gave him a hug. "Hi, Richard. Is there no Sophie today?"

He shook his head. "She's up to her ears with funeral arrangements and tending the store, but she sends her love."

"Let her know if she needs help. I can come over." She gestured to her computer. "It's on, so you can surf the Internet. Take all day if you want. We've got four cruise ships in, and I'll be helping the crowds of customers looking for a bargain." She smiled and departed.

He sat behind Anika's desk and glanced around the office, tastefully decorated with colorful Scandinavian artwork and a framed photo of Anika and Mike on their wedding day.

Richard had four hours between charters to try to solve the mystery of the stranger. On a hunch, he decided to first check on Mike's disturbing account of probable murders of Marine and Army vets.

He keypunched onto a site given him by Mike and checked out the most recent murder victim, a Force Recon Marine named Jack Hawkins. Jack had joined Richard's four-man fireteam during Richard's final months in Afghanistan. They'd gone on several missions together.

Richard remembered Jack as a compact, wiry man of few words, deadly with a knife. Richard shook his head in disbelief that anyone had gotten the better of him. He was the type who snuck up on fellow Marines on lookout and put his knife to their throat, then whispered something like, "Good thing I'm on your side or you'd be dead meat."

The Internet site indicated that Jack died four days before the stranger showed up on St. Mark. Investigators' initial conclusions were that he had slipped and hit his head against the stone edge of his backyard pool, then fell unconscious into the water and drowned.

Richard exited the site, texted Jack's wife, Bonnie, and told her he had heard that her husband had passed away. He added that, in his judgement, Jack was the best of men, and that he was sorry to hear of his passing.

Surprisingly, she responded immediately, thanked him for his words, and declared, "It wasn't an accident. The house curtains were open that night and Jack had plenty of light to guide him. I would dearly love to personally kill the son of a bitch who bushwhacked my man."

Richard wrote back, "I'm looking for a pattern and may even have a suspect."

"Good. Tell me when you cut the bastard's throat."

Richard continued to search for another half hour, learned nothing new, and decided he'd gotten all he could from the Internet. He reviewed the bits and pieces he had learned from Mike Stiles. Both victims were decorated, combat-hardened Army or Marine veterans who had served in Afghanistan. All received honorable discharges and had been living normal civilian lives, with wives, kids, and good jobs.

Richard found a pen and wrote on a blank piece of copy paper:
Stranger
Military trained
Ruthless.
He stared at the three words and connected them with lines.

The man had the instincts not only of Force Recon training but of a sniper. Those guys could stalk right up to your boots without you seeing them. The man's attacks on Sophie justified 'ruthless.'

He penned another entry on the page:
Why Sophie?

He added the names of the murdered men, wrote *The killer*, and drew lines to each victim. Finally, he drew a dotted line between *Stranger* and *Killer*.

He chewed on his theory that the Army and Marine deaths were murder and that they might be connected. Mike had described the circumstances of their deaths, and Bonnie had convinced him that Jack had died not of an accident but of murder.

But, hell, thousands of US military personnel had served in Afghanistan. People die. Some by murder but more from natural causes and accidents. Why should anyone believe those few were murdered, and by the same man?

Because they all served at the same time. The same time Richard was in country. Could he be the missing connection? *Could I be a target?* That was a logical conclusion, but the stranger was not attacking him – the stranger was attacking Sophie.

He pondered that most bewildering question of all – why Sophie? The best answer Richard and Sophie could come up with was that the stranger was after Sophie for some reason connected to Cliff, her violent ex-boyfriend.

From what Sophie had recounted of her doomed relationship with Cliff, he had made his share of deadly enemies in the world of international crime. Maybe one of those enemies hadn't heard that Cliff was dead and decided to murder Sophie as revenge against Cliff. Anyway, that was their working theory. She had no other enemies.

Richard also wondered if Sophie knew something that made the stranger feel threatened. He and Sophie had explored that idea as well, with nothing gained. But if he, Richard, was the common denominator in this madness, maybe Sophie was under threat because of him. That thought set his stomach to churning.

As he rose to leave, another even more troubling scenario popped into his head and he wondered why it hadn't arisen before. The stranger could be attacking Sophie as a diversion, while his actual target was Richard.

CHAPTER 22

Sophie's walk back along the track from the Coxons' to the paved road was not nearly as eerie as the walk in. Though she still felt the jitters when she and Maren paused at the fallen tree, her hands barely shook.

Maren frowned. "God, look at that splintered end, like it was exploded. Hmm, blackened and burned around the splinters. Well, George and Michael will need to chop it up to move it off the track."

Sophie pointed to the remaining stubs of a dozen small branches, most of them buried in the ground but several fully exposed. "I hadn't noticed those before. Their tips are cut at an angle."

"They look dangerous, like spikes. God, Sophie, they're at the lower side of the trunk, where it struck the ground, to stab whoever the tree fell on."

Sophie shuddered. "They would have killed me!"

"What's this?" came a booming voice from the track, ahead of them.

George approached and stared at the tree. "Damn, it looks like it was blown in two by a cannon."

Sophie said, her voice shaking, "The stranger did it and I saw him, the man who attacked me before. He intended this to happen. It wasn't just to scare me – see those branch stubs?"

He examined the exposed tips, then touched Sophie's shoulder, his eyes questioning.

She said, "You don't have to tell me. I promise to get you or Michael to come with me next time."

George nodded. "It's best for now, Sophie, until we kick the guy off our island." He turned to Maren. "Things were quiet at work, so I thought I'd come home in case you needed help on the funeral arrangements."

Maren said, "I'm glad you're here. I'm okay with the arrangements, but I'm getting frightened of what that man will do. He's a danger to the island."

George approached the splintered stump and poked and sniffed. "It smells like burning and chemicals."

Sophie asked, "Is it gun powder?"

"Sort of, yeah." He picked up a mangled piece of plastic. "I think he attached an explosive to the bottom of the tree and detonated it as you walked by."

"I had paused."

"Hmm. But he detonated it anyway." He looked at her, eyebrows raised in question.

"He wanted to scare me?"

"Could be, but I believe he wanted to kill you, and thought you'd continue walking. His timing was off and your pause saved your life." He put the plastic in his pocket. "Let's get back to town. I want to talk this over with Richard."

When they arrived at the store, a half dozen people stood in small groups under the shade tree and conversed quietly. They turned toward Sophie and the Coxons as they approached. People listened to Sophie's tale of her sad discovery of Uncle John's body.

She decided not to mention the latest attack and was thankful that George and Maren followed her lead. People needed to feel the loss and remember the good of Uncle John.

Richard emerged from the store and shut the door behind him. He approached and gave her peck on the cheek. "Sad days."

She nodded. Took his hand and led him aside. Leaning close to him, she described her dangerous encounter on the trail. "George met Maren and me as we came into town. He said it looked like an explosive caused the tree to fall."

He caught George's eye, and George approached. Reaching into his pocket, George handed the plastic shard to him. "There was more, but this was the biggest piece. I believe he wanted to kill her."

Richard turned the plastic over in his hand. "Right color, right material. Looks like a shaped charge. Just right for cutting a tree in half. Probably remotely detonated. C-4 most likely."

Sophie said, "He waited back in the woods until I approached – my gosh, that meant he saw me leave the store and ran ahead to set his explosive."

Richard frowned. "He might have been watching you from the time you arrived this morning. Maybe he was in the store last night. Did you see anything inside that looked out of place?"

"No," Sophie said, thinking back. "Wait. Yes. There were dusty footprints on the floor. Two of them, with tread marks, like your hiking boots make but a different pattern. They weren't there when I left yesterday evening."

Richard grunted. "I think it was the stranger."

"Oh my gosh! You don't think he killed Uncle John, do you?"

Richard shook his head. "I don't know."

Maren joined them and seemed to have heard the last part of the conversation. "From what Uncle John said to Sophie yesterday, it seemed he knew he was going to die, and he chose here instead of a hospital."

"So, we don't really know," Richard said. "But it does look like whoever this person is, he was there. He could have waited in hiding, saw Sophie and the others arrive, guessed – or knew – that Uncle John had died, and decided to ambush Sophie."

Sophie said, "I agree, and if he saw me start up the road, it was a good guess that I was on the way to the Coxons. It seems he's been spying on us all week and has figured out who we are and where we go."

The others nodded, faces grim.

Richard turned to George. "I don't quite agree with your thought that the stranger wanted to kill Sophie. I believe he wanted to terrorize her."

Sophie asked, "Terrorize?"

Richard looked at her. "That's his pattern. Think about it. He could have ambushed you and me, or George and me, when we were in the valley. I felt his eyes on us." He glanced at George.

"He saw us," George said. "It gave me a creepy feeling. I wish to hell he'd shown himself instead of hiding like a coward and coming after you."

"He may not be a coward," Richard said.

"You think he's following a plan?" George asked. "He wants to scare the hell out of Sophie? Then what? And why? What's in it for him?"

"Maybe he's after me and attacking Sophie to divert our attention."

George shook his head. "Why would he come after you?"

"I have no idea, but there have been several mysterious deaths of men I served with or were in a unit near mine in Afghanistan. Mike Stiles told me about their deaths, and we're convinced they were murders, not accidents.

We don't know why, but the last death was only a few days before the stranger arrived on St. Mark. It could be coincidence, but I'm getting the feeling that whoever murdered those men is the same man who has been lurking on our island."

"You've got a point," George said. "But it seems to me more likely than one of Cliff's former enemies trying to murder Sophie. Bottom line is—you're both at risk." He looked Richard in the eye. "It's just a thought, but you two could drop out of sight for a while, off island. He'd have no choice but to leave."

"Sorry, George. I don't think that's a good idea. I need to find him now and turn him over to the police before someone gets hurt. Otherwise, he'll either take out his anger on someone else, or simply wait until we return and take us by surprise."

George's lips quirked. "Why did I know you'd say that?"

CHAPTER 23

Richard followed Sophie into Uncle John's room, along with George and Maren. They gazed silently at their friend's blanket-draped figure. Richard shut his eyes and said a prayer for the gentle man's soul.

Sophie said, "I've gone through Uncle John's things. As you can guess, there isn't much. Mainly, it's clothing, but there *is* this." She opened a drawer in the armoire and retrieved a cardboard shoe box, which she set on the small table. "It seems to be the only personal thing in his room, though it could contain only a pair of shoes. Anyway, I thought we should all be here when I opened it."

"Go ahead," Maren said quietly. "There may be instructions in addition to his will, maybe things we should forward to his relatives."

"By the way," George said, "did anyone call his next of kin?"

"I did," Sophie said, glancing at Richard. "I talked with his brother on Richard's sat phone. His name is Paul, and he lives in Baltimore, where they grew up. He's flying down. Graham Walters said he'll give him a ride on the helo when he and the medical examiner come tomorrow morning."

"Is there a will?" George asked.

"I don't know," Sophie said. "But Uncle John mentioned a lawyer on St. Thomas. He mentioned a name – "

"Borresen?" George asked. "Arthur Borresen? He's the lawyer most of us use. He's a good man, and not too expensive."

Sophie nodded. "Yes, that's the one."

"I can give him a call," George said. "I know him pretty well. He may want to come as well to read the will and pay his respects."

Richard said, "I'm sure Graham will be okay with another passenger."

Sophie said, "Shall I open the box?"

Everyone nodded and she lifted the lid. "Well, it's not shoes." She removed a billfold and an envelope that contained photos of what appeared to be family and soldiers, which she passed around. On the bottom was a wooden box.

"That looks like something he'd have bought at a bazaar in Afghanistan," Richard said.

Sophie removed the fitted top and handed a packet of folded documents to Richard.

He opened and scanned through each. "This is his DD214 form, his honorable discharge from the Army."

Richard noted the date and Maren remarked, "Twenty years ago. He arrived here right after he left the Army."

"Must've had it all planned out," Richard said.

"He didn't want to return to Baltimore," Sophie said, and when she noticed the curiosity in everyone's expressions, she added, "He told me last night that he'd reported an underworld theft of valuable property where he worked. They were going to kill him for that."

"Was that why he joined the Army?" Richard asked.

"Yes."

Richard continued scanning the documents. "Orders – after boot camp, then Army infantry training, Ranger School – I'll be darned – then a couple of Stateside tours, quartermaster school –"

"What's that?" Maren asked.

"Supplies and distribution," Richard said.

George nodded. "Sounds like it'd be useful stuff to know if you wanted your own little store."

Richard murmured, "Two tours in the Middle East. Hmm, for some reason, he was assigned to an infantry company. A combat unit. I recognize it. Yeah, they were still in Afghanistan when I was there. A good outfit."

"But it sounds like he was doing infantry duty," George said. "Why didn't he do something with supplies?"

"Hard to say," Richard said. "He'd had a couple of quartermaster assignments back in the States. Let's see. He was sergeant by the time he arrived in Afghanistan. Maybe he was getting restless. Wanted to use his Ranger training."

He looked at the next document. "Well, here's something. A commendation and a medal. Jeeze, the Medal of Honor! That's the highest medal there is, awarded for combat bravery. Listen, "for conspicuous gallantry...risk of his life above and beyond the call of duty...rocket fire...small arms fire...ambushed convoy...withering enemy fire...covered the withdrawal of wounded soldiers...saved the unit from being overrun by the enemy...""

Richard looked up, a tear in his eye. "This is as brave as it gets. And he survived. Many – maybe most – Medal of Honor winners die. They cover a grenade, or they keep fighting until the enemy shoots them. Our Uncle John was a combat vet. A real hero, and so modest he never told anyone."

"I had no idea," George said.

"He was totally quiet," Sophie whispered, looking at his draped form on the bed.

"Quiet but brave," Maren added, reaching down and touching the blanket.

Sophie replaced the contents and returned the box to the armoire. "I guess we should let people pay their respects."

Maren said, "I can take the first turn as host."

Richard glanced at Sophie, who seemed hesitant. "We can have a little coffee at my place." She nodded, and everyone moved through the store, into the morning sun.

Richard turned to George. "I'm sad about him."

"Me too, but what a life and in the end he lived a happy twenty years. Everyone took to him and he loved being their honorary uncle. Especially the kids. Jenny was in tears when she heard he'd passed away. Michael looked pretty broken up as well."

"Are you going to work?"

"Yes, if only to hang out with the guys and tell stories about Uncle John."

They shook and George headed through town. Maren gestured for folks to enter to pay their respects. Richard caught Sophie's eye and she came close. He gave her a gentle hug and they strolled hand in hand to his bungalow.

He asked, "How are you doing?"

"Not too well. I keep thinking I didn't do enough for him."

"He was really sick."

"Right. From what I understand, they could have kept him going for a while if he were in the hospital."

"We know that's not how he wanted to die."

"True," she said, stifling a sob, "but I wish he could still be here."

Richard gave her a squeeze and they walked closely enough for him to smell her scent, feel the brush of her shoulders and hips.

"I do, too. He was one of the really good people."

"Anyway, I'm a mess."

"Well, you're doing the right things, Sophie. You thought to get Maren to help out and you called Paul."

"Yes, but forgot to ask George or Michael to go with me when I went to get Maren."

At the bungalow, Sophie made coffee. Richard opened his safe and hauled several firearms and cleaning gear to the kitchen table. Sophie set down steaming mugs and sat opposite him.

Richard field stripped his Glock and arranged the pieces on a clean cloth.

Sophie said, "This is how you calm your nerves, isn't it?"

"Yeah, I think so. The guns need a coat of oil to protect them from salt air, but I guess this is as much for me as for them."

He tipped his oil tin to a rag, but only a drop came out. Sophie rose. "I know where the new can is inside the safe."

When she returned with the oil, she lay another weapon on the table and looked at him with haunted eyes. "I found this. I hope it's okay I unwrapped it. I was curious."

Richard frowned. "I've never shown you?" He reached to pick it up but, seeing her terrified expression, withdrew his hand. "What is it, Sophie?"

She whispered in a deliberate way, as if speaking out loud would break a dangerous spell. "This looks exactly like the stranger's knife. Where did you get it?"

Chilled by her reaction, Richard grasped the sheathed weapon, attempting unsuccessfully to recall details beyond those he now spoke, "A guy gave it to me in Afghanistan, right before he returned to the States."

CHAPTER 24

He lay on his stomach on the mountain above the town, twenty feet from where he'd hidden the previous times, to avoid creating a pattern. He still had the exact view he wanted – the store, the town, and Drake's cottage.

He had come directly from the tree debacle, saw the girl arrive at the store with two friends, then half the town showed up. Obviously, the old guy had died. Good, now he could push forward with his mission. Full speed ahead – get done and freaking *leave*.

Drake and the girl walked through town holding hands. So those two were not just friends. Probably one reason Drake was so anxious to acclimate to the rainforest area of operation. The guy had to be pissed that he'd messed with his woman.

The two of them disappeared into Drake's place, stayed less than an hour, then the girl wandered back to the store and Drake appeared ten minutes later outfitted with hiking boots, canteen, and daypack. It looked like he was going to roam the island. *That should take at least two hours, which gives me all the time I need.*

He waited for Drake to climb the mountain and be well away. Mosquitoes and other insects sucked blood and sweat from his exposed skin. People visited the store and came out wiping their eyes. As always, no one even glanced up to where he lay. Around noon, the crowd thinned and then the street was completely empty. *Lunch time,* he figured.

He rose on hands and knees, and scanned three-sixty. Seeing no living thing except two chickens off to the right, he lowered himself to his belly for the downhill journey to the Marine's bungalow.

After a full hour, he rose amid the tall grass surrounding the bungalow and approached a back window, casually reaching inside to release the simple latches, open the jalousies, and slither in. He remained silent. Drake might have snuck back, or he could have a pet.

Probably not a dog, because he'd have taken a dog on his walk. Maybe a cat. A snake. The sniper chuckled at that last choice. Nah, if that guy had a pet it would be a German shepherd, trained to kill. Freaking Marine, go figure.

He sniffed the air. There was no tickle to his nose, which meant no animal with hair was living with Drake. Careful not to touch anything, he tiptoed out of the bedroom to the living room, and then into a compact kitchen. To the right was a bathroom. It was a nice place, kept militarily tidy. Just like the other two vets, though wives probably did the housekeeping for them.

He conducted a methodical search for where Drake kept his arms and ammo. All military types loved pistols and rifles, in fact, anything that could kill or blow someone up.

He tramped across the mat floor covering, listened for the hollow sound of a wooden trap door. Heard only the thump of his boots. Until he reached a spot next to Drake's bed. There was a space of three feet between the bed and the wall, sufficiently wide for storage. He folded the mat back, and smiled.

Fitted neatly into the concrete floor was a steel box, its top flush with the floor. He knelt, leaned close and smelled a trace of gun oil. He ran a finger around the joint between the hinged top of the box and its body. Felt a rubber gasket, and nodded in professional approval. The box was sealed tight. He'd still need to oil his arms, but sealed, and if he added a desiccant, corrosion would have a hell of a time establishing itself.

He sat back on his haunches, picturing pistols, ammo, maybe night vision goggles, and a couple of knives. *The one I gave him?* He glared at the four-digit combination lock. He had no clue how to get past that, without damaging it or the contents of the box. Which for his own reasons he did not want to harm.

He replaced the mat, deciding on a more satisfactory way to gain access to the box, and realized this day was looking up.

CHAPTER 25

Richard set a grueling pace, mulling over the loss of Uncle John. He had been a humble man with a generous spirit. That he had served in the military in combat had come as a surprise to Richard, and the Medal of Honor had blown him away.

He wiped sweat from his brow, pushed himself harder, trudged upward along a deer track, oblivious to bird calls, to the rustle of breeze in the tree tops. God, what a missed opportunity to share their common bond.

Richard swore in frustration. Did humility sometimes go too far and extend into prideful secrecy? No, that was too harsh. Not confiding in Richard was John's choice. Come to think of it, who had Richard ever shared his battles with? Jimmy Franklin and Mike Stiles, of course. They shared war stories, along with the emotions of combat, from the highest to the lowest.

Why had Richard never shared with John? *I must have.* Well, he'd shared with George, his best friend, at least that one night on the porch, the two of them sitting and listening to the insects, staring at the stars. Yeah, he'd shared with him. Of course, he'd shared the PG version with Sophie, which she told him was as much as she wanted to know.

But with John? Richard had assumed word would filter over to him, but then again, those conversations with Jimmy and George were in confidence, man to man. He paused and caught his breath, a wide swath of grass before him, sea breeze ruffling his hair. He walked forward, onto the promontory, toward the edge, where the sense of height tickled his stomach.

Waves crashed a couple hundred feet below, pounded ancient rocks, fueled the blow hole. Catching his breath from the steep climb, Richard stepped back and admired the view. He decided he'd been as humble or as secret as John. Either one of them could have made the first step. *But we didn't and now it's too late. We're both old coots who should have shared,* he concluded.

We had so much in common. Not only the searing experiences of combat, but a code absorbed by those constantly facing violent death. Such as the idea of participating in, and contributing to, a mission bigger than yourself. Sacrifices made and rewards received that transformed a person's soul.

He abruptly turned, strode across the waving grass and entered the bush. He continued west, keeping to the high ground, his mind immersed in following twisty deer tracks. He pushed himself and heightened the challenge by taking shortcuts across switchbacks, to prove he could navigate without the help of an established path.

Richard maintained a constant altitude by remaining perpendicular to the slope of the land and simply following the contours of the mountain. He could circle the island in this way, but after an hour he changed direction and emerged on another swath of grass, this one the size of a football field.

The natural folds and gullies had been smoothed over a dozen years ago to form a landing pad for helicopters. Helos were the preferred mode of transportation for the owners of the half-dozen walled compounds on the North Side, facing on the Atlantic.

Richard thought of those folks, rich or famous, who chose St. Mark because of its isolated beauty. Mountains separated them from the other islanders and their town and modest homes. In fact, the various owners kept to themselves, with only the occasional cocktail party with other North Siders. Sometimes, they ventured into town for a sunset dinner at Pirate's Rest.

Both groups – islanders and rich folks – got along well, respecting each other, perhaps each seeing in the other a common love of their surroundings and appreciation of their privacy and independence. Richard knew a number of his friends who worked for North Siders, either in yard maintenance or as cooks, and all seemed delighted with the income and happy with how they were treated.

He personally knew only one North Sider, Judge Santiago Valdez, son of an aristocratic Spanish family and President of the International Criminal Court in The Hague. For him, St. Mark was a retreat from the stress of his high-profile position.

The judge's cases almost always involved international figures accused of crimes against humanity. They were powerful and ruthless men who occasionally tried to assassinate him. But he was protected twenty-four seven by two officers of the special operations group of the Spanish National Police Corps – the Cuerpo Nacional de Policía.

Richard walked the paved road from the helo pad along the North Shore, with compounds and the Atlantic Ocean on his left, the bush and mountains on his right. He turned at the judge's compound and took a key out of his pocket for the iron gate.

A muscled, large-framed man in tropical khaki uniform approached from inside the compound. He returned Richard's smile. "*Hola,* Señor Richard."

"*Hola,* Pablo. I didn't know you arrived." He replaced the key in his pocket.

"Yes, we arrived early this morning." Pablo opened the gate, and shut it again after Richard passed through. "We all love the blue sky and blue ocean and the warm air."

"Is the judge up and around?"

"Oh yes. He is finished with lunch."

Richard continued to the house, where Miguel, who doubled as cook for the judge, waved Richard in. He was short, wiry, and dour, and gestured for Richard to remain in the foyer.

Richard admired a reproduction El Greco painting on the whitewashed wall. The faint hum of a generator came from outside the house. Miguel reappeared and motioned Richard through. "He will see you now, *señor*. Would you like something, perhaps a beer or wine?"

It was an invitation Richard knew came from his host, a man of old-world courtesy. "Thanks, Miguel. A beer would be nice."

Miguel nodded and led the way down a familiar hallway to the great room.

When they arrived, Miguel paused and said, "*Señor* Drake." He waited for the man inside to rise from a chair and nod to him, then departed.

Richard extended his hand, "Good morning, Judge Santiago."

They shook and the judge gestured to the chair next to his own. The seating arrangement faced a wall of French doors, beyond which lay a lawn and the Atlantic. They sat, quiet for a moment, because the judge was a methodical man and not to be hurried in anything he did.

"Ah, Richard. It is good to see you."

"Thank you, judge. Welcome back." Richard studied the man he helped protect, about fifty-five years old, balding and heavy set. There were black smudges under his eyes.

Miguel appeared and silently set a glass of beer next to Richard, who took a long, thirst-quenching drink.

"I think," the judge said, "looking at your clothes, that you have been alone this morning. Walking with your usual vigor in the midday heat, if I am not mistaken by the small amount of beer remaining in your glass."

Richard marshalled his thoughts and said, "You are correct, sir. Two things have happened you should know about."

The judge nodded, made eye contact, then gazed out the window, ready to listen. As he never hurried himself, he never hurried others.

Richard continued, "The first is that John Parker has passed away."

"I'm sorry to hear that," the judge said. "I knew Uncle John. A very good person."

"We'll all miss him. He died in his sleep last night, most likely of heart problems. Folks are arriving from St. Thomas this afternoon or tomorrow to take care of formalities. It's a sad day for us."

The judge nodded.

"Sir, the other item is possibly related to your security. An intruder arrived on the island several days ago. He has stalked Sophie and attacked her twice. Fortunately, she escaped harm."

"*¡Dios mío!* This is your friend, who I have met. A lovely young woman."

"Yes." Richard described both attacks and then said, "I have reconnoitered the valley twice. I believe he is a military veteran, well versed in fire arms and explosives, and extremely dangerous."

"Do you have any idea what this man's motive is? Why he's threatening and attempting to harm Sophie?"

"Our best estimate is that he's an assassin sent by an enemy of Sophie's ex-boyfriend – Cliff Webb – with instructions to terrorize and then kill Sophie as revenge against Cliff. He must be under the impression that Cliff is still alive. There is also a possibility that he is after me, and the attacks on Sophie are a diversion."

"Or that Sophie and you are both diversions?"

"Like the last time?"

"In a way. At first, it appeared only Sophie was a target."

"This could be similar. You could be in danger. I know you just got here – "

The judge waved a dismissive hand. "I will not run from such people. You have warned me. Pablo and Miguel will deal with this man should the occasion arise. What is your plan?"

"I have become familiar with the valley, and tomorrow I will learn more about the man himself. I hope to discover the location of his base camp. Next, I will return with Jimmy Franklin, who you have met, and we will capture him and turn him over to the police."

"If he resists?"

"If he attacks, I will shoot to kill."

"Has he threatened others on the island?"

Richard shook his head. "Only Sophie. He was in Uncle John's store last night, but appears not to have harmed him."

"You think he meant to damage the store as a further threat to Sophie?"

"Yes. But he held off because of Uncle John being there, obviously very sick and unable to save himself."

"Then his focus does appear limited to Sophie and to material things, but not to other people."

"So far, that's true, but I think you must remain at highest alert, sir. I will brief Pablo and Miguel and keep you updated."

"I agree with your plan."

Richard recognized that the meeting had ended. He stood and extended his hand. The judge stood and they shook.

"Take care, Richard. You are too valuable a friend to lose."

"Thank you, sir. I will."

Richard briefed both guards, then walked the paved road to town. He was famished, and went directly to his bungalow.

At the front door, he looked for the telltale that he always placed between the edge of the door and the door frame, exactly two fingers below the latch bolt. A tiny folded piece of brown wrapping paper should have been there. He looked down. Stooped and picked it up.

He paused and wondered. It could have been Sophie picking up something she'd left, or a friend, poking his head in after knocking and receiving no answer.

Or someone else.

Richard assumed someone else. Carefully, he pulled the door open. Listened. Only the normal daytime cicadas outside, a dog barking in town.

He entered. Again, paused. Sniffed. A trace odor of sweat – a sour, locker-room smell. He checked the main room, kitchen, bedroom. Everything was in its place.

Richard checked the windows. All fine, except the back window in his bedroom. The metal latch of the twin jalousies, which connected and locked them, was fully pushed home, locking the two halves. But it was not twisted into its downward position. It stuck out. Richard always twisted it down.

He thought back. Had he left the latch like that because he was in a hurry? Had Sophie opened and then shut the jalousies, maybe not in the habit of twisting the latch down?

The fact was, either could have been the case. Out of curiosity, he flipped the grass mat back to expose his arms safe. He squatted and examined the face, the combo lock. He dialed the combo and opened the door. All looked exactly as he had left it. He secured the door, replaced the mat. Stood.

His gut screamed, *it was the stranger.*

CHAPTER 26

The next morning, Sophie met Richard at the Coxons' after breakfast. The family were getting ready for church service in Pirate's Rest while she and Richard were going to pick up guests at the helo pad. Their walk through the bush to the paved road still gave her the chills, especially when they passed the chopped-up remains of the tree that nearly killed her.

Richard had parked a car he borrowed from Judge Santiago on the road and they got in, Sophie feeling a little disoriented after walking everywhere for months. The sensation deepened as they zoomed along at thirty miles per hour, trees whizzing by on either side.

The speed reminded her of her past life in Florida, where she traveled everywhere by car, rushing here and there, always in a hurry to complete the day's endless to-do list. She preferred St. Mark. Her home.

"This is a Land Rover Defender 110," Richard said with enthusiasm. "In case you're wondering."

She smiled to herself and poked him in the side. "Richard, you've already told me that."

He laughed. "She's a little clunky. Definitely not a Porsche. Jeeze, I haven't driven in two years. Surprised I still know how. It's fun."

"You like driving?" she asked. "To me it's just a way to get places."

"I love driving. I even drove an Army tank once."

"Hmm. I'll stick with wind surfers and my good friend's sailboat." She looked out the window at the passing bush as they crossed the mountains that bisected the island from east to west. They curved left, with the villas of the North Siders rushing by on their right.

He patted her leg. It felt good, his touch. He turned left and parked where the island's single road ended at the helo pad. They climbed out and ambled to the grassy field.

Up a gentle rise stood an abandoned lighthouse, near the very western end of the island. Beyond the lighthouse was where Richard took her for target practice, a wild place of breaking waves, black rocks, and continuous wind. She could almost smell the tang of the spent bullets, the tinkle of casings as they fell to the stony ground. *Happier days.*

The helo showed up as a tiny dot over Jost Van Dyke and grew as it approached. She turned to Richard, raising her voice above the wind, "Have you ever driven one of those?"

"Not yet. Little airplanes yes, but not a helo. They take both hands and both feet." He laughed. "I might not have enough coordination."

"If you can take apart and reassemble your Glock blindfolded in the blink of an eye, I'd say you could fly a helicopter."

"Thanks, Sophie."

"But I'm still a better shot."

He guffawed, and said something smart, but the arriving helo blocked it out. She pushed him anyway and he laughed.

As the helo settled and doors opened, she returned to the real world of Uncle John's parting, and all the sad duties of death. Graham Walters from the police department and a doctor had arrived on Saturday to take care of formalities, including confirmation that Uncle John had died of natural causes with no indication of foul play. They had also discussed burial at sea, and said they'd take care of the paperwork approving that.

Now, the pilot remained inside as two men emerged. As soon as they got close to Sophie and Richard, the pilot waved and lifted off, banked and curved back to St. Thomas. Sophie almost jumped when the first man got close. He was a thinner version of Uncle John – the same kind eyes, sandy hair, and large, capable hands. He gave her a little smile, eyes twinkling in recognition, and they shook. His grip was firm, his hands damp.

"You must be Sophie," he said in a quiet voice. "I recognize you from the picture John sent me. I'm Paul."

"Hi," Sophie said, wiping away a tear. "Sorry. You look like your brother."

"People say that. Couldn't tell us apart when we were kids." He waited for Sophie to collect herself, and lifted his hands. "Sorry for the sweaty handshake. That was my first ride in a helicopter."

The other man patted Paul's thin shoulder. "No worries. I'm scared to death of the things. Been on a dozen rides, and it doesn't help at all. Thanks for sitting up front. It let me grip the arm rests and keep my eyes tightly closed."

Paul nodded. "That's good to hear."

Richard said, "Arthur, this is Sophie Cooper. Sophie, Arthur Borresen, Uncle John's lawyer."

Sophie and Arthur shook.

He looked to be in his mid-fifties, had a paunch, bushy white eyebrows, white mussed hair, and sunburned face. "Hi, Sophie. Maren always says good things about you. She and George have been my friends for years. George and I argue about whose ancestors got to the islands first. Mine were Danish merchants."

Sophie chuckled. "And his were pirates."

Arthur squinted as if delivering a confidence, "Yes, they were all in the same line of work."

Richard said, "We were thinking of coffee and breakfast at our local place, called The Pirate's Rest. We could talk there."

All agreed and piled into the Land Rover. Conversation was muted as Richard drove, and Sophie figured that reality was settling in for Paul. She turned to him. "Have you been here before?"

He shook his head. "No. John and I corresponded. He never wanted to return to Baltimore, but we always figured I'd make it down one of these days. He said I had an open invitation. I'm an engineer with the city, and we're understaffed. It never seemed the right time to take off." He blinked.

She touched his shoulder. "I know what you mean. We knew he had health problems, but never guessed we'd lose him."

"I'll sure miss him," Paul said. "He loved it here, running his store and being friends with everyone. His letters were full of island news, stories about the kids, and good words about you helping him out and – how did he phrase it – oh yeah, how you 'brought a breath of fresh air into my life.'"

"Thanks," Sophie said, "but I think he helped me more than the other way around. Anyway, I'm glad you came. For yourself, and for Uncle John's memory. I'm glad we got a chance to meet you. And Uncle John's invitation is still open. Come and visit."

Richard slowed the car as he descended the road toward town, and he stopped at the store. "This is where John kept all of us supplied with what we needed. We can take a look now or later, if you'd like, Paul."

Paul gazed silently. "He sent me a picture. I would like to visit. Let's take care of business first, I think. Get that out of the way. And the service. I understand he'll be buried at sea?"

"Yes," Richard said. "That's unless you'd rather take his remains to Baltimore for burial. We all agreed that you have the final say."

"Let's bury him at sea," Paul said thoughtfully, looking at the store. "Like I said, he never returned to Baltimore. He'd rest peacefully here." He looked at Sophie. "Among his friends. Those who loved him for who he was."

"Okay," Richard said. He continued the drive into town. "We've made tentative arrangements for the burial and service later this morning. I'll let folks know you gave the go-ahead."

He parked in front of The Pirate's Rest. Inside, they sat around a table. Arthur ordered a full breakfast. Paul ordered toast.

Arthur removed a set of pages from an envelope. "I can start off, if you would all like." He paused for nods. "Good. My main job for John was to record his will. He told me what he wanted it to say and I put it into legalese. His wishes were simple. I won't bore you with reading the entire document. You may feel free to read it yourselves." He set the pages in front of Paul.

Paul said, "Go ahead, Arthur. I'll read it later."

"Okay. He assigned me as his executor, and I'll look after issues like probate, notifying Medicare, Social Security, and the Veteran's Administration. The will is simple. There are two beneficiaries. Sophie and Paul."

He looked at each and they nodded. "John gave the store to you, Sophie. The land, the building, the inventory, and the corporate bank account, with a balance of approximately five thousand dollars. As an aside, he told me that before you came the balance had always been negative."

Paul said, "I'm glad he gave you the store, Sophie. From his letters, it was clear he thought of you more as a daughter than a friend or employee."

Arthur smiled. "Good. Paul, you are named as beneficiary on two life insurance policies and his savings account."

"Oh," Paul said. "Well, that's generous."

"It's a substantial amount. He took out both policies when he joined the Army." Arthur looked Paul in the eye. "You might want to know that you were the original beneficiary, Paul."

"Not our parents?"

"No, you." Alfred tented his hands. "I hope I'm not out of place by sharing this among – "

Paul waved a hand. "Please. We're all friends – valued friends."

"Alright. John told me during each of our face-to-face meetings that you were the world's best big brother. Especially, when he was threatened by unsavory people from the docks, where he worked. He told me you did lots more than give advice. You stood with him when the going got tight."

Paul nodded, appearing embarrassed.

Arthur continued. "Especially, when they pounded on the door the night before he left for boot camp."

"It was the thing to do."

"John said they had guns."

"Yeah, well, I had a baseball bat."

"Good man," Richard said.

Arthur smiled, made eye contact with Sophie, Paul, and with Richard. "There you have it. Paul, I suggest you read the will, and if anyone has any questions?"

Paul scanned the will and handed it to Sophie, who read the three pages. *My goodness*, she thought. *He gave me his store. I have a solid place on the island. In the community.*

Muted conversation at the door brought her back to the present. "Oh, I guess we should go. People need to set up for the reception, and we need to get ready for the service at sea."

CHAPTER 27

It was almost noon and Sophie stood on the rolling foredeck of CAPRICE, outside the harbor, surrounded by every other boat on the island.

Uncle John's casket rested on a wide board, set crosswise on deck. Sophie and Michael took their places on one side and George and Maren on the other. Father Rex, the island chaplain, stood at the head of the casket, Bible in hand.

Richard tended the helm and set the engine on slow-ahead. He'd left the masts bare, and turned CAPRICE into the swells, so that the rolling changed to gentle pitching. Judge Santiago was back there, sitting on the edge of the cockpit, along with one of his friends from the North Side who Sophie had not met.

The judge's guards sat amidships. Both had calmed down since the service ashore, during which their eyes constantly darted about for threats to the judge. Sophie now realized why the judge almost never came to town – his security team went crazy.

As the flotilla closed around CAPRICE, Father Rex raised his right hand and crossed himself, as did about a third of the folks there. Chatter turned to silence. All gazed at Father Rex. Witnessing their respect and love for him, Sophie decided to start attending his Sunday services.

To the sea sounds of water lapping against hulls, the chiming of halyards against masts, and a lone seagull, Father Rex read the burial service. Hymnals appeared, and everyone sang about 'those in peril on the sea.' Not a dry eye remained.

At a signal from Father Rex, Sophie and the Coxons raised the board, and the coffin slid into the sea. It floated for several moments and then descended, hazed to an ever-duskier sapphire hue and disappeared into the deep. Sophie handed flowers to Michael, who lay the colorful blooms on the swirling water.

The boats returned to the harbor and moored to the pier, either to one of the ten cleats or to an adjoining boat. Gradually, chatter and little jokes emerged as people stepped ashore and made their way to The Pirate's Rest.

Sophie walked with Richard and the Coxons. She found herself glancing about for that one missing face – Uncle John, pausing and smiling among friends. For a moment she felt his presence, and was washed with his spirit, but only briefly. She mostly felt sad and was relieved when the reception wound down.

She and Richard ambled over to the store. She felt close to this man. Treasured him. He was a tough guy, but also tender. *Like now, holding my hand.*

"Are you returning to the valley?" she asked.

"Yes, first thing tomorrow. I want to check my gear today."

"Take care, Richard."

"I will." He leaned closed and kissed her. "Will you be okay here?"

"Yes. I'll try to think of all the good times with Uncle John. I'll sure miss him. I'll wait here for George to walk me back to the Coxons'."

They kissed at the door and she watched him walk down the street toward his bungalow. After a while, he turned, as usual, and they waved their good-byes. *Yes, he's got a tender side.*

She entered the store and propped open front and back doors with stones. The breeze chased out the stuffy air, but not her feelings of loss. Uncle John was so much a part of the store and yet now he was missing.

As she absently straightened boxes and cans, grief descended again, unhindered by friends and chatter. She had wanted to leave the crowd, but being alone didn't help, and there would be no shoppers on a Sunday.

Sophie gritted her teeth. *Enough pity party.* She fluffed her hair, glanced around the shelves, and strode up and down the aisles. She stepped around a boxes ready to be arranged on adjacent shelves.

She gazed up and down the aisle. Peered closely at the boxes on the floor. Recalled that pirate ancestor of George, and suddenly knew how she would spend the rest of a lonesome afternoon.

She admitted that what she planned was not in the spirit of dear Uncle John. But it was in perfect harmony with the temper of that rogue from the eighteenth century.

CHAPTER 28

Back at his bungalow, Richard changed into hiking gear. In a daypack, he loaded fifty rounds of Glock 17 ammo, his Iridium sat phone, a multi-purpose tool, rations for a day, mini-light, poncho, first-aid kit, and few other items that might come in handy. Into a pocket, he stuffed a length of brown twine. On his belt he mounted knife, Glock, and canteen.

Of all his gear, Richard placed the highest value on his knife. While some of his comrades carried exotics, like scaled-down machetes or massive Bowie knives, Richard opted for the Marine-issue Ka-Bar. It was the opposite of flashy, with its modest 7-inch blade and stacked leather-washer handle. But it was combat proven.

He, like most Marines, sprayed the blades, guards, and pommels with flat-black paint, which protected against corrosion and made the weapon nearly invisible at night. Richard unsheathed his Ka-Bar, checked the blade with his thumb and smiled grimly. If it came to close combat, this is the weapon he wanted in his hand.

He quickly ate a sandwich, set the usual telltales, and exited his bungalow. He trudged straight up the mountain, leaving other homes behind. After entering the bush, he continued north, then crossed the paved road and hiked east.

He soon arrived at the same entrance to the valley as before and he gazed down at the canopy, penetrated by the tall trees and wreathed in a shifting mist. He reached into his daypack, retrieved greasepaint camo, and applied green and brown to face and hands.

The descending path was steep, and as usual, grew slippery as he approached the valley floor. A drizzle started, but he figured getting wet was the least of his worries. When he reached the valley floor, he instinctively heightened his attention to sights and sounds.

Richard shifted his thoughts to the mission, which was to find a way to locate the stranger when it came time to track and capture. On the face of it, the task was daunting. With his military training, the stranger could easily evade a determined search by dozens of men in the dense foliage.

But Richard had formed a plan, the first step of which was to entice the stranger into trailing him. Departing the deer track, he navigated between valley wall and creek, keeping one or the other in sight to ensure he maintained a generally southward route.

He recognized only two landmarks within the rainforest. One was that magnificent tree from which George never cut a limb. The other was the black boulder outcropping where the stranger made his backup camp. Everything else appeared as a monotony of dense thickets, tall trees, and wide-leafed plants.

He made his way down the west side of the valley, remaining in the open, baiting the stranger to follow. When he reached the black boulder, he didn't bother to mount the stone ladder. He paused only for a moment, then continued south.

Richard knew the stranger preferred night operations, which meant that now he was probably there in the valley. Likely, he gathered sleep in a series of daytime catnaps. When awake, his highest priority must be to watch for intruders.

The man would certainly peer out from within the boundaries of his camp and he would also conduct patrols around the camp and further afield. The last time Richard had been in the valley, the stranger had spotted himself and George for sure. The time before, he had certainly tracked himself and Sophie.

That formed a pattern of the man maintaining a vigilant watch. So, after an hour of roaming, Richard was confident his prey had picked him up and was now skulking in the bush, keeping tabs.

At the southern extreme of the valley, with the sound of the waterfall loud in his ears, Richard changed course and eventually arrived at a familiar glade. To one side stood that other tree George had shown him. It was actually a good landmark because of its distinctive forked trunk, and the stub of a branch that became a piece in a boat, and the business end of a wicked booby trap.

Richard strode to the gap in the bushes. He inspected the foliage on either side, looking for the straight lines of parachute cord. There were none. He knelt and carefully felt for trip wires. Again, nothing. *The bastard probably set it up somewhere else.*

He stood and felt a tingling between his shoulder blades. *The stranger. He made the mistake of looking directly at me and just gave himself away.*

Richard imagined his enemy as having relaxed when he saw Richard examining the site of his trip wire. Perhaps he congratulated himself for moving it and envisioned his trap working the next time, taking Richard down.

Richard made a show of rubbing his jaw, as if puzzled. He peered around the glade, wearing a frown of frustration. After a full minute, he walked through the gap.

On the other side, he angled left, toward the valley wall, and when he was twenty feet away he angled so that his route paralleled the wall, heading north. He increased his speed to gain a lead. He didn't bother to hide his trail on the rainforest floor. In fact, he lightly scuffed leaves and stepped on the odd twig to mark his passage.

After ten minutes, Richard reached a clump of dense bushes with a gap wide enough for a person to pass through. Conscious that his lead was only half a minute at best, he immediately knelt, pulled out his length of twine, and strung it across the gap at a height of two inches. He tied the twine to bushes at either side of the gap, forming a trip line. He covered it with leaves, then continued through the gap.

Ahead, Richard spotted a wide plant, and slithered beneath its umbrella-like leaves. He lay on his stomach facing the gap and he waited. Seconds later, a figure in a ghillie suit arrived, blending almost perfectly with the surroundings.

Certain he had the stranger actively tracking him, Richard backed out from under his leafy hide and sprinted in the same direction as before, away from the other man. He figured the trip wire and his increased speed would buy him the time he needed.

With concealing forest behind him, Richard angled sharply to the right and soon reached the creek. He stepped into the flowing water and moved upstream, placing his boots only on submerged stones, and not on the muddy bottom, to hide his route.

After two hundred yards, Richard exited the creek to a distance of fifty feet He walked parallel to the running water and when almost at the place where he had stepped into the creek, he hid behind a tree.

Richard heard the stranger before he saw him. He risked a look. The man walked quickly and glanced down often, tracking the scuffed leaves that revealed Richard's trail. The man stopped cold when the trail ended at the creek. He emitted an audible curse.

The man peered in all directions, then commenced searching in ever-larger circles about the spot where Richard had entered the water. After the third circle, he stood still for a minute and finally shook his head, his expression one of frustration. He departed toward the northwest and Richard followed him back to the creek.

The man stepped into the creek and waded upstream. Richard followed on land, concealed by foliage. After twenty minutes, his quarry paused at a fallen tree with full, leafy branches. Its upper half lay in the creek and the rest on shore. The man stooped and maneuvered under the branches. He remained out of sight for a full minute, then emerged carrying two one-gallon plastic jugs filled with water.

Richard grinned and quickly averted his gaze. *This is where he gathers water for drinking, cooking, and washing.* It was a place he must visit every day or so, perhaps even more often.

Following him now without giving himself away was impossible because crossing the creek would cause too much of a delay. Too bad, because Richard wanted to locate that base camp. Reluctantly, he watched as the man turned north then east and disappeared into the bush.

He was glad to have found the watering place, but now felt the burden of planning and executing the next phase of his plan. Theoretically, execution was straight forward. Making it succeed in practice against a trained and motivated enemy was less than certain.

CHAPTER 29

He awoke with a start, bathed in sweat, imagining Drake peering down at him. He realized it was a dream, but he continued to lay perfectly still, listening to the nighttime noises, willing his heart rate to return to normal.

Just a nightmare, he assured himself. Furtively, he reached for his night-vision goggles and breathed a sigh of relief when he found his base camp its usual self, bathed in shades of NVG green and empty of Drake.

His watch read a little after nine o'clock. No worries. He had plenty of time. After gulping water and munching a pack of field rations he thought back on the day, beginning with climbing out of the valley and patrolling its rim. At the seaward side of his circuit, he'd spotted a motley flotilla at the mouth of the harbor. With binoculars, he'd witnessed the burial at sea, which must have been the old guy in the back room of the store. So he had died, as expected.

It was time to continue what the old man had interrupted – burn the freaking store to the ground. Continue to distract Drake. He turned his thoughts to the bothersome Marine, and admitted that he was rattled by Drake's incursion into his valley that morning.

That guy was way past being meddlesome. *Hasn't he realized he can never find me? Truth is, a hundred of him couldn't find me.* But several paces further on, he frowned. *I lost him in the end.* The Marine had set his little delaying-action trip line, went on to lay his trail, then disappeared.

True, it was not particularly imaginative, walking through the rocky creek. *Hell, that's what I do. It works, that's the point. Bottom line, I couldn't pick up where he climbed back onto dry land.* He must've backtracked. Yeah. Retraced his own footsteps, then dodged sideways and out of the valley.

What Drake had been after, he hadn't a clue. He'd paused at the backup camp, but did not ascend as he had before with that other islander. Their discovery made the camp useless as a hide. He'd have to transfer his supplies to another location. Or maybe not. Hell, he'd blow the store and let it burn, killing the girl. Then on to Drake, and he was done. No reason to shift all that gear.

He rose and gazed through the rim of bushes at the surrounding rainforest. All normal. He checked his ghillie suit, brushed off twigs and folded it neatly. For his mission that night, he favored mobility over stealth. Instinctively, he reached to his belt and felt his Afghan *peshkabz*, its bone handle comforting. *Damn.* Talk about a proven fighting weapon. *I'd love to get into a knife fight with that guy. I'd gut him in two strokes.*

Gathering what he needed, he descended to the rainforest floor and hiked out of the valley, through the bush, and settled into a vantage point two hundred feet uphill of the store. As before, only a sliver of moonlight illuminated the hill and he was glad to have the NVGs.

Through gaps in the foliage, he saw lights in the cottages. In time, lights blinked off at the bar. A man staggered out and wove his way down the street and up the hill to one of the cottages. There were angry words between him and a woman, and a slammed door. Then, only the cicadas, a whispering breeze, and waves beating time against the rocky shore.

As he lay on the lumpy earth, he sensed his own impatience. He'd come this far on his journey and was thankful this was the last of a series of annoying tasks. *This whole exercise is turning out to be a pain in the ass,* he reflected. Especially the waiting.

He thought about his short but eventful career as an Army sniper. *It is truly amazing how much time I have spent waiting for a target to appear. Prone in the dust like a dead man for a day, maybe two days, simply to gain my three-second window, center him in my sites, and squeeze the trigger.* Well, on this final mission, he had made two clean kills to date and only two remained. The waiting was almost over.

Just before midnight, he descended to the store. He entered through the unlocked back door. Glanced at the empty bed in the back room. Moved into the store, past the counter and its ancient cash register.

The jalousies were closed. Faint moonlight leaked through the cracks, but only enough to hint at darkened aisles and shelves holding ill-defined merchandise. He had stowed his bulky NVGs and reconnoitered with a penlight, masking most of the lens to illuminate only what he needed to see. A person never knew whether a sliver of light might show through the jalousies, get spotted by a busybody islander, and bring someone to check for problems.

He found what he was looking for on a shelf running along the far wall – kerosene in one-gallon cans. The islanders used it for their lanterns to light their homes. He didn't smoke, didn't have a lighter, and he realized he'd left his matches back at camp.

No problem. He could find matches easily enough in the store, preferably some of those kitchen matches with sturdy wooden sticks. They'd remain lighted long enough to do the job. Get a little fire going.

He searched the outside aisle with no luck. There was soup, cereal, all sorts of other crap, but no frigging matches. He curled around to check an inside aisle. Paused when he heard a dog bark in the near distance. Then continued, slowly, methodically. He glanced ahead and abruptly halted.

The aisle was nearly blocked by stacked cardboard boxes. He tapped one with the toe of his boot, but it was heavy and remained stubbornly in place. Full of canned food. Yeah, this aisle was all canned stuff. Beef, Spam, vegetables. No matches. *Hmm, well, check it out anyway, to be sure.*

He squeezed sideways to get through the gap between boxes and shelves. His knife caught on one of the stacked boxes and he pushed ahead. The box shifted and there was a distinct click.

What the hell?

He continued forward, heard another click, and the entire right side of the aisle seemed to fall away. He raised both arms to shield himself from an avalanche of rakes and shovels, and *holy shit*, a dozen cutlasses. They tumbled down and clattered onto the floor.

With his arms effectively occupied fending the tools from whacking into his torso and legs, he stood defenseless when multiple objects swung out of the dark and smashed his head.

They remained around his face, his ears, the back of his head, lolling back and forth as he attempted to brush them aside with his shoulders. No go. His forehead and ears throbbed. Liquid ran down his face. Blood? He had no idea.

He'd dropped his penlight and was blind to details. He did make out that those were four small cans that brained him. All dangling from strings. Must've been visible all along, but who would have thought to look up at the ceiling?

The last of the tools and cutlasses clattered to the floor and now formed a tangled barricade to his further progress. He touched the dangling cans. One was open. Damn. He felt holes. *Was that liquid from inside the cans?*

He thrashed out in a rare temper, whacked the cans, but in the dark they swung back like little demons, hitting him again. He stopped and drew a breath. Raised his arms to head level to keep them away.

He retreated in a blind fury, cursing under his breath, leaving the cans swinging, the tools piled on the floor, his penlight lost somewhere.

Abort the mission, he muttered. *That must've awakened the entire population. Time to get the hell out.*

He exited through the back door, sprinted half-way up the mountain, and looked down. Lights came on in near-by cottages. Doors opened. Puzzled voices called through the insect noise.

He kept going.

"Damn that girl," he said out loud. "She'll pay."

CHAPTER 30

The next morning, Sophie walked to town with George and Michael.

At store, she asked, "Could you wait for a minute? I want to make sure everything's okay."

"Sure," George said.

Michael smirked, "Are you going to check your mystery project?"

She gave him a look. She needed privacy, not two guys looking over her shoulder. Especially, if something had gone wrong.

But he would not be put off. "You're bugging us, Sophie. Let us in."

She laughed and gestured for them to follow.

Michael squirmed in first and let out a low whistle. "Whoa, what a mess. Like a deer went wild in here. Look at that pile of tools."

Sophie said, "Yesterday, I set a trap to spill the tools and – see those dangling paint cans?"

"With one dripping yellow paint?" George asked.

"Yes. They were aimed at whoever set off the trip wire that released the tools."

Michael circled around and began replacing the tools. "Must've been noisy."

"I'll check with customers," Sophie said. "Ask if anyone heard."

George said, "Deer didn't do this. Must've been the intruder. No one else would have come in after you'd closed for the night."

"Yup," Sophie said, examining the paint cans. "I set it for him. Hey, look! I think there's blood on this one. Good."

"Good?"

"He tried to kill me – twice."

George shrugged. "I guess. But shouldn't we leave the combat to Richard?"

"I'm showing that coward – two can play his game."

Michael grinned. "Give 'em hell, Sophie."

"Well, he's gone now," she said. "See you guys later. Thanks for picking everything up, Michael."

"Sure."

George tried to look serious. "Just take care, Sophie. See you this afternoon. Come on, Michael, we have a boat to finish."

Fifteen minutes later, Richard walked in, gave Sophie a kiss, and peered around. "You look chipper this morning."

"I am," she said. "I set a trap for the stranger and he ran into it."

"Oh?"

She gestured toward the aisle. "It's all cleaned up now, except for those hanging paint cans."

He gave her a sly smile. "I was wondering about the paint cans."

"Right. See those boxes?"

He nodded.

"They take up half the aisle, so when he – "

"He?"

"The stranger."

"Damn."

"Anyway, when he moved sideways to get past the boxes, he pushed one, which activated a trip line to let all those tools fall down."

"Must've made a helluva racket."

"That's the idea. To startle him. Since he's military and used to sneaking around, he wouldn't panic. He'd freeze for a moment to think what to do next and listen to hear if someone moved outside."

"Okay," Richard said, touching one of the dangling paint cans.

"Those paint cans were tied back, high in the ceiling, and they released at the same time as the tools."

"Clever. You tricked him into a kill zone."

"Kill zone?"

"A place where defenders can shoot attackers, and the attackers are stuffed together and can't defend themselves."

"Ha. Well, it was dark in here and only took a second for the paint cans to swing down – into the kill zone – and whack the schmuck in the head."

"Remind me never to get you mad."

She raised her arms in goal-post position to flaunt her biceps. "That's right, bud."

He grinned and inspected the cans. "This one has a leak."

"Yup. I poked holes just above the level of paint, to let it splash out when the can hit him. Now his clothes and body are stained bright yellow."

"Maybe it'll stick. Make it easier to find him in the rainforest."

"Maybe, but I picked latex, which makes cleaning up the floor lots easier, so he may be able to wash the stains off."

Richard examined the cans. "Did you see this? It looks like blood."

"Right, I think that sharp joint between the body and the top of the can wounded him."

"There's some on the floor, too. He was really bleeding." Richard gave her a hug. "Sophie, you are amazing!"

"Thanks," she said, and hugged him back. "Hmm, you look like you're going on a hike. One of your morning tours of the island?"

"Yes, I want to check out the North Side coast for clues to how he got here. I'm thinking he arrived by boat. I'll stop by and update the judge as well. See you when I get back."

He kissed her good-bye and left. After a hundred yards, he turned and they both waved.

Alone inside, her glow of victory was tempered. There was still an hour before customers showed up, and the store had a lonely feel again. Plus, that damned man was still lurking out there. Determined to cause mischief, or worse.

She needed something to keep her busy. The aisles were pretty much stocked, and the list for the ferry was up to date. Maybe there was something else she could do to fight back.

CHAPTER 31

By the time Richard hiked to the judge's villa, the air had warmed, well on its way to mid-day hot. Pablo stood in the shade of a palm tree outside the gate and gave Richard a lazy smile, only his watchful eyes hinting at his constant attention to duty. "*Hola,* Señor Richard."

"*Hola,* Pablo."

Pablo shifted in the shadow of the palm tree's narrow trunk, sharing the scant shade. "Any news on the mysterious stranger?"

Richard joined him and shrugged. "I hiked through the rainforest yesterday and got on his trail. He's good. Moves well, knows the usual tricks and a few more."

"*Que lastima.*"

"Yeah, a real pity. But I did follow him, looked for a pattern."

Pablo's grin showed his white teeth. Again, the eyes.

Richard continued, "He stopped along a creek where a tree lay half in the water. He disappeared into a hollow formed by branches and leaves."

"A hiding place, perhaps?"

"Yes, it's where he stays out of sight while he collects water. Apparently, when he passes nearby, he stops and fills one or two plastic jugs and carries them to his base camp. Then, when he's going out, he drops off empties."

"So now you know, and you can find him."

"Yes."

"Perhaps the judge will ask me to volunteer to accompany you, *mi amigo.* I would cherish the opportunity to, what is the expression, 'hone my skills'?"

Richard clapped him on the shoulder. "I wish, Pablo. But the judge needs you here."

"It is fine, *mi amigo*. I see the island women coming and going to their jobs and have a word with them."

"And admire their, er, figures."

Pablo chuckled. "Yes, they know, and they walk with that certain sway, just for me."

"You're a good man, Pablo."

"I know, *Señor* Richard," he said with humor as he unlocked and opened the gate to the judge's villa, "and you as well."

The judge had finished breakfast and was reading a thick document. He and Richard shook hands, the dour Miguel hovering in the background.

"Ah, Richard. How are you this fine morning?"

"Hello, Judge Santiago. I'm fine, thanks. I hope all is well with you."

"Oh yes. The Hague seems far away."

Richard nodded at the document in the judge's hands. "But the work continues?"

"Ah, a little light reading. Will you join me with a coffee?"

"No thanks, judge. I'm on my way to the northern shore, looking to see if the intruder has left a boat."

"Good thinking. And if you find the boat?"

"I will leave it. As much as I'd like to see him arrested, I don't want to make him desperate. He's already dangerous enough. But if I find the boat gone, then I'll know he's gone, and I'll call Graham Walters. He'll send the Coast Guard out and hunt him down."

"You think he is dangerous to others?"

"Could be. If he's trying to harm Sophie, then my bet is he's harmed other people in the past."

"But not judges?"

"I don't think so." Richard rubbed his chin. "He seems focused on Sophie. Last night, he was in the store and tripped a booby trap she rigged up. A couple of paint cans hit him in the head."

"*¡Dios mío!* Miss Sophie is a wildcat I think."

"She is. Oh, one more thing. Following our previous meeting, I found that someone has been inside my home."

"One of your telltales?"

"Yes. It was out of place. A faint smell in the air too – of a sweaty person."

"You think it was that man?"

"That's my best guess. But why he was there, I don't know."

"Did he see you with Sophie? Perhaps, he considers you as a danger to his plan to frighten her."

"Could well be."

"Well, thank you for this update. Good luck today, Richard. You will be careful, I am sure."

They shook hands and Richard departed. He made his way down the paved road, and when it turned right, toward town, he crossed, continued east, and entered the bush. He walked several hundred yards, passed the final villa, and emerged on the rocky northern shore.

Before him, the undulating Atlantic stretched to the horizon. Next stop was the States or Bermuda. He worked his way along the shore, weaving among palm trees and desiccated bushes, all bent from the wind.

Richard kept his eyes open for a beach or a protected cove, where a boat could be pulled ashore and stowed. He passed two small beaches and inspected the land above each. He found only driftwood, tangled lines, and floats for fishing nets. The usual.

At the third beach, he spotted a pile of palm fronds. *Maybe natural, maybe not*, he thought as he approached. He removed several palm fronds, revealing a folded-black rubber rectangular object. He pushed the remaining fronds aside and unfolded what turned out to be the sides of a deflated rigid inflatable boat – a RIB.

Richard searched for an identifying name or number and grinned when he found a four-by-six inch blue and red sticker. Emblazoned was the name, 'All-Island Boat Rentals,' along with a St. Thomas address, serial number, and phone number. He dug out a pen and notebook from his daypack and copied the information.

He had heard of the rental outfit, located about three marinas to the west of Red Bay Marina, his base on St. Thomas. He called with his sat phone.

A man answered. "All-Island Boat Rentals."

Richard introduced himself, said he was working with Graham Walters of the St. Thomas police.

The man gave his own name as 'Al' and said, "Never heard of Graham Walters."

"I'm investigating a case on St. Mark."

"St. Mark? Do people live there?"

"They do, and someone who appears to have rented one of your Zodiac RIBs is visiting the island right now."

"Hmm. What's his name?"

"That's what I was wondering. He's been bothering some of the residents over here. I'm trying to locate him and kick him off the island."

"Jeeze, he's got one of my boats, all the way up there? Just past Jost Van Dyke, right?"

"Yep. It's a nice boat, a Classic Mark II Zodiac." Richard read him the serial number.

"Hell, you're right. That's one of my boats. Outboard, too?"

Richard glanced around, spied a low mound of branches and rotten coconuts. He lifted a branch and said, "Yeah, the motor's here."

"Damn. He told me he needed a tender to get to and from a friend's boat anchored off Red Hook."

"Well, he's here now."

"And you're sure the boat's okay?"

"Yep. I'm standing right next to it. Looked it over. Deflated, covered with palm fronds, no tears or leaks. Did he give you his name?"

"Sorry, uh, Richard. I can't give that information out."

"How about I have the police give you a call and verify that I work for them?"

"Hell, I don't know. It's a privacy issue, man."

Richard had about enough of this guy. "How about I ask a police patrolman visit you with his siren screaming and blue and red lights flashing? I could arrange that."

"Whoa, buddy, don't get worked up. I'm just trying to protect my customer."

"He's a dirt bag, Al. He lied to you and he's bothering people up here. You'd be better off trusting me and keeping me on your side.

You'll probably need my testimony when he steals your boat and motor."

"Alright. You work for the police you say?"

"I'm their representative on St. Mark. Sort of a deputy. Call and check, Al. Just dial 911."

"No, that's fine. Let's see. Yep, here he is. I copied all his driver's license info. Name's Tim Keller."

Richard scowled. *Where have I heard that name? In the Marines?* "Did Mr. Keller pay by credit card?"

"Yeah, with the same name, if that's what you're going to ask next."

"Can you give me his address?"

"Rather not."

"Sure. I'll have Graham call you and you can tell him. He'll figure out a way to prove he's a policeman. Anyway, Keller's address is in the States, right?"

"Yeah, New Jersey. Uh, say, where's the boat now?"

"North Side of St. Mark, out in the boonies. No one around. It and the motor are covered with leaves and branches. Both are above the high tide mark."

"Out in the boonies, huh? Any risk of someone stealing it?"

"Not a chance. I'll tell you what, Al. If Keller doesn't ride off the island in this boat, you know, if the police take him off in handcuffs, then I'll call you back, help you locate it."

"That would be great. Richard, is it?"

"Yes. Richard Drake. I'm a charter captain, keep my sailboat at Red Bay Marina."

"Okay, captain."

"Richard."

"Right. Okay, Richard, much appreciated. Gotta go – customer waiting."

Richard disconnected and stared at the boat and motor. He let his gaze wander over the dry bushes and trees, out to sea.

Who in tarnation is Tim Keller?

He searched in a widening circle. Found a cache of supplies under another pile of palm fronds. He was tempted to cut the RIB to prevent the intruder from escaping, but, as he had told the judge, it was better to leave well enough alone. There was too great a chance the man might hurt someone while attempting to steal an islander's boat.

CHAPTER 32

By the time Richard reached town, he was seriously hot and thirsty. The sun was high and not a drop of water remained in his canteen. He was hungry, too, for real food, not field rations. He glanced inside the store, hoping to entice Sophie out to lunch. She sketched him a wave but added a discrete shrug, meaning she was committed to a conversation with a customer. He continued through town.

Passing The Pirate's Rest, his sat phone buzzed and he figured that was all the excuse he needed to enjoy a big burger, fries, and cold beer. He settled at a table on the deck, careful to choose a place with shade, and pulled out his sat phone.

It was a text from Bonnie Hawkins, the wife – now the widow – of Jack, the fellow Marine who had supposedly accidentally tripped and drowned in his home pool. Bonnie wrote: "Still nothing new on Jack. Life goes on, I guess."

Richard called her, mainly to let her know she had a friend during this tough time.

She answered on the second ring. "This is Bonnie."

"Hi, it's Richard Drake."

"Oh Richard, thanks for calling."

"Not much new down here either, though I'm still looking into that intruder who's been terrorizing my girlfriend, Sophie."

"He sounds creepy."

"Yeah, that's the word for him. But Sophie's a fighter, Bonnie, like you. She rigged a booby trap in her store."

"Oh my!"

"Yep. The guy was snooping around and got hit with paint cans. Drew blood."

"You're right, she has spunk. No wonder she likes you."

"Thanks, Bonnie. Oh, the guy's name is Tim Keller and he uses a New Jersey driver's license for ID. Ring any bells?"

"Tim Keller," she said, rolling the name over as if to squeeze meaning from it. "You know, that sounds familiar. Maybe Jack mentioned him. Yes, I think he did when he came home from his last deployment to Afghanistan. I can't remember what he said. I'll let you know if it comes to me."

"Okay. It could help." Remembering Sophie's remark that his Afghan knife was the same style as the stranger's, Richard said, "It's a wild hunch, but did Jack bring back an Afghan knife, you know, as a souvenir?"

"Why yes, it was like a dagger. He kept it on display above his desk. The last time I looked, it was gone. Maybe he packed it away."

Richard felt a chill. *Did Keller steal the knife? If so, why? Was it valuable?* "Let me know if it turns up, okay? It may be important."

"Sure. Thanks for calling."

He disconnected with a feeling of something lurking in the back of his mind. *Maybe I should talk with Mike.*

He keyed in Mike Stiles' number.

"Hey, Mike, it's Richard."

"Where are you? Stopping at St. Thomas today?"

"Not today. I'm focused on untangling the mystery of that guy who's terrorizing Sophie. I hit a little pay dirt today. He arrived in a Zodiac, which he stashed on the North Side. It's a rental, and I called the number on the agency sticker. Turns out the guy's name is Tim Keller."

"Tim Keller, Tim Keller. Was he in Afghanistan?"

"Yeah."

"Wait, I remember a sniper named Keller. Yeah, Tim Keller. A real loner."

A mental vision of the man popped into Richard's head. "Right, me too. Definitely a sniper. He accompanied my unit on a couple of ops, sometimes alone, sometimes with a spotter. Left us after we got into enemy territory. Had their own mission I guess. Okay, that's a connection, Mike. The intruder is Keller, who operated in Afghanistan and mixed with local Army and Marine units."

"Did you check with the wife of that other Marine?"

"Just got off the phone with her – Bonnie. She recalled Keller's name, and when I asked, she said Jack brought home a souvenir – a knife similar to the one the guy used when he attacked Sophie. Funny thing is, Sophie said Keller's knife looked just like mine from Afghanistan."

"Damn. Richard, did all you guys go to the same bazaar?"

"No." Again, that chill, this time of recognition. "It just came to me. I received mine as a gift."

"From Keller?"

"I think so."

"You're thinking Keller gave knives to the murdered guys?"

"Yes, and then decided to steal them back."

"Maybe they're valuable."

"Right, could be museum pieces. The important thing is, we know he's after the knives and he's come to St. Mark for mine. He steals the knives and kills the owners, erasing links between himself and them and the knives. As far as Sophie goes, I'm guessing Keller thinks she knows too much, just like the guys he's murdered."

"And he wants to distract you, make you think she's his target, keep you off guard."

CHAPTER 33

Still nursing his wounded military pride and intending revenge, especially for the sliced cheek from the freaking paint can, Keller let himself through the back door, into the old guy's bedroom. This time, he was careful to shine his shaded penlight all around for booby traps. Everything appeared normal – stacks of boxes, from soup to diapers.

He ghosted into the store, past the counter, and stood still. He absently rubbed his fingers along the three rough stitches in his cheek. Blood still oozed, but he'd doused the wound with anti-infection crap, so it should heal okay. He'd be out of this hell hole in a day, two at the most, and would find a doctor to neaten things up.

Keller brushed a hand through his hair and felt something between his fingers. Yellow flakes of dry paint shown in the beam of his penlight, triggering a scowl and a shot of adrenalin. *Heaven help that woman when I get her. I'll make her suffer. Tie her to a termite nest. I wonder if they'll eat her, like ants do. Start with her eyes. I'll stick around to see that. Have to gag her, I guess.*

He pushed the pleasant image out of his head and focused on his real plan. It carried little risk and promised to cause an effective distraction while he attended to his other task. Plus, it was quick. He'd be off the island by the following morning.

He scanned the ceiling with the penlight, noted the heads of a half dozen nails protruding and recalled the swinging paint cans. Next, he inspected the walls, shelves, the closed front door, and shuttered jalousies. As before, nothing appeared out of place.

He skipped the near aisle and the next one over because he knew what he wanted was not there. Kerosene had to be somewhere. This dip-shit island had no electricity. They needed kerosene for their old-fashioned lanterns.

Walking down the third aisle, he played his penlight over a neat row of six one-gallon cans of the stuff. He ran his hand across the smooth surface of the cans. The corners of his mouth turned up slightly, about as near as he got to a smile.

He set a compact explosive charge and detonator behind the cans. If the blast didn't kill the girl, the resulting fire would. It would be a quick death, without the nibbling termites. Too bad, but he had to move forward. He raised his penlight and took a step backward to check that his handiwork was not visible. He lightly bumped into a display of cleaning fluid.

Heard a click.

Distinct.

Metallic.

With his brow furrowed in puzzlement, he swung around and stared at a slightly displaced can of cleaning fluid. Then he heard another sound, like lots of little balls falling and rolling. *What the hell – ball bearings? These people don't need ball bearings!*

He aimed his penlight down. Around his boots flowed a stream of – not ball bearings – but shiny, multi-colored glass marbles, cascading out of the lower shelf, bouncing onto the wooden floor, and flooding the aisle.

"Damn, damn, damn," he gasped, his voice too loud, as he instinctively stepped away from the continuing stream of marbles, seeking clear floor.

He shined his light at the ceiling, half expecting more paint cans. That maneuver, and his retreating back foot stepping onto marbles, upset his balance. He reacted instantly, leaning his weight on the front foot. But it was too late.

His back foot rolled away from him, his legs spread, arms now frantically scrabbling for support.

There was nothing to grasp. The shelves were burdened with boxes and bags, all of which were loose.

Flailing desperately, he tipped backwards and crashed onto the sea of marbles. His head snapped against the floor.

He saw stars, then nothing.

*   *   *

Keller blinked. *My God! I've been unconscious!* He checked his watch. It was nearly five-thirty, only half an hour till sunrise. *I've been out cold for three hours.* He pushed himself to a sitting position. He sensed moisture dribbling down his cheek and felt with his fingers. Blood. The fall must have jerked the wound open.

Leaning forward, ignoring the hundreds of marbles poking painfully into his butt and legs, he sat upright. He located his penlight and surveyed the scene.

Yup, a whole bunch of marbles. He cleared a spot and stood, then pushed flat-footed through the damned things. He checked his explosive charge and its detonator. All was set. Obviously, the marbles hadn't made much noise, nor did his fall, or meddlesome neighbors would have discovered him. For once, luck was on his side.

Keller departed the store and trudged upward toward his observation spot. He predicted his wait would be short.

CHAPTER 34

When she arrived at the store the next morning, Sophie asked George and Michael to come in with her.

I need company.

She scanned cluttered shelves and rustic walls. Before, they echoed John's kind spirit, his absent-minded manner. But since the space had been violated by the stranger, walls and shelves radiated haunting unease.

She opened jalousies to let in sunshine and sea breeze, but the air remained oddly fetid, like bad breath. Stifling a shiver, she approached her handiwork from the previous afternoon. She was conflicted in what she wished to find.

On one hand, she hoped that awful man had tripped her second booby trap, and she fantasized that he would still be on the floor, injured but completely capable of being hauled off to jail for attempted murder. However, she dreaded another confrontation with her attacker, and the other half of her mind hoped to find the trap untouched.

Nearing the far aisle, down which her trap awaited, Sophie's hand began to shake. *Vulnerable. That's how I feel – like being in a dream, naked in public, except a thousand times worse.* Before she could steady herself, another emotion shouldered in – *revenge.*

God, Sophie. Get a grip. How about 'justice'?

Was justice an emotion? No – nor was revenge. But revenge was what surged through her muscles and bones. *Kill the bastard.*

Revenge. What a primeval, uncivilized notion. Very Old Testament, 'an eye for an eye.' Surprisingly, it felt good, because she was fighting back. Both her booby traps were fighting back. But harming another person felt beneath her fundamental self. She saved people, like she saved Jenny from the sea, those months ago.

Did Richard think of revenge when he studied the rainforest battleground? Or was he driven by justice? He was a Marine, someone who meted out punishment. But not necessarily revenge. He said he and his comrades believed in their cause, but their goal was to subdue the enemy, not get revenge.

Maybe justice was his motivation. *But not me,* she thought. *I have been threatened in a personal way, not like a Marine facing a nameless enemy. For me, for this minute, I own revenge.*

Sophie turned into the aisle and spotted dozens of marbles on the floor. Her trap had been sprung. She turned and caught George's eye.

She pointed and said, "Watch out."

CHAPTER 35

Peering at the store from up on the mountain, Keller munched his last field ration and drank the last of his warm water. He watched two men depart. The girl remained inside, completely exposed to explosion and fire.

Would she die at once or would she become trapped by debris, only to succumb to smoke inhalation, or better yet, to witness the flames approach, blister her flesh, and devour her life? At this stage, he told himself, he did not care, as long as she died and severed the dangerous link between himself and the knife that Drake now held.

He let the moment drag on, that special window when the sniper's planning, furtive observation, and patient waiting paid off with opportunity. He reconsidered, and decided that he *did* care how the girl died. *Slowly and painfully.* She had been a royal pain in the ass. Besides, her pain was Drake's pain, and he was a pain in the ass as well, so screw him.

At length, he grasped the detonation transmitter, removed the safety cover, and pressed the button. Instinctively, he ducked to avoid the shock wave, though he kept his eyes sufficiently above the grass and rocks to view the store. He'd earned it.

Destruction on a violent and all-encompassing scale was instant and complete. The wooden walls blew outward, disintegrating into pieces and falling. The corrugated steel roof popped up briefly, then individual sheets skipped and cartwheeled in all directions and landed with satisfying metallic whacks.

Surprisingly, shelves and their burden remained standing except for those close to where he'd planted the charge. The thick wooden counter in back of the store was still in one piece, though its support at the end nearest the charge was missing. The counter tilted toward that end, and belatedly the ancient metal cash register lost its grip and slid down into the now smoldering rubble.

Tendrils of smoke rose in the rubble field, then the overheated, kerosene-splashed wood caught fire. The flames at first were tentative, but quickly blossomed into hungry yellow tongues.

He heard yells of alarm from near-by cottages and a bell clanged in town. It was time to depart. He paused for a final look at the burning wreckage, the billowing smoke. He sniffed the acrid stench. He heard a hollow pop and then more, and figured it was canned goods overheating and exploding.

He scrambled up the mountain and into the concealing bush. *One down, one to go.*

CHAPTER 36

Richard heard the explosion as he departed his bungalow on the way to an afternoon charter. He looked to his left, and his gut tightened at what he saw. Wood and then sheets of roofing blew skyward and fell. A plume of gray smoke formed.

He dropped his gear and sprinted down the path to town. Someone shouted to him and he pointed to the store, pouring on speed.

Had Sophie been inside?

George, Michael and a half dozen boatyard workers poured onto the street.

George's face was ashen. "We left her only twenty minutes ago. All was fine."

Men rushed into the fire station, tugged on jackets and boots, clambered onto the Jeep 'fire engine."

"It's the damned intruder!" Richard yelled, over the noise of the Jeep and a gathering crowd.

He broke into a dead run, his entire focus on Sophie. He had to get there quickly. She might need immediate help. He glanced around for Jimmy, with his ever-present medical satchel. Didn't see him. *Damn.*

Richard outpaced George and the others, everyone except those with cottages nearby. A hundred feet from the store, the fire engine passed him, horn blaring, men shouting for people to get out of the way.

The vehicle skidded to a stop and two men unreeled fire hose. Richard dashed past and waded into the flaming wreckage, feeling heat through his deck shoes. *No matter.*

He feverishly navigated debris strewn between still-standing shelving. An exploding can whacked his left ankle. He scanned the aisles. *No Sophie.* He worked his way toward the back, increasingly concerned. *Had she gone out?*

He reached the counter in back of the store. A glance into the lightly-damaged back room told him no one was there. He heard a noise and gestured for approaching fire fighters to freeze. They stopped, hose in hand.

Richard knelt and shut his eyes, listened through the crackle of fire and approaching voices.

"Help."

God. Sophie!

He peered beneath the sloping counter and saw her in the shadows. He squirmed in, brushed away debris, placed his hand on her shoulder.

"Sophie, it's me. Are you hurt?"

"Richard! I can see your lips move but I can't hear anything. Help me."

He folded himself next to her in the cramped space. He heard the rush of water behind him, the hiss of steam. He tenderly felt Sophie's arms and legs, then her torso. All seemed fine. He leaned inward and felt her head. Again, no wounds. Saw her eyes blink, her lips move. Felt her arms reach out for him.

Supporting Sophie around her shoulders and under her knees, he carefully slid out from under the counter. He saw fire fighter boots on either side, and slid further, making room for helping hands.

"Support her whole body," commanded a gruff voice. "There may be broken bones. Keep her back straight."

Outside, a fire fighter stood by a stretcher and they placed Sophie down gently.

Her eyes had been closed and now they opened wide, taking in the concerned faces around her.

"I think I'm okay," she said in a shaky voice. "I was stooping down to pick up a can of tomato sauce and everything went black."

She began to rise, but the gruff guy put a hand on her chest. "Not yet, Sophie." Richard glanced and saw it was George, tears streaming down his cheeks.

CHAPTER 37

Keller was in a foul mood as he slipped and slid along the muddy trail down the west wall of the valley. *I never should have paused.*

Yet he had. He had entered the bush, but the delightful sounds of anguish from islanders and the clanging bell of their two-bit fire company pulled him to a halt.

Then, he couldn't help himself – he was compelled to return, to view the catastrophe he had brought down on the girl and Drake. Hell, no one pursued him. He was in no danger.

Keller had remained to witness the initial arm-waving confusion. It was a true delight. Then he spotted the damned Marine tear through town and into the burning wreckage. He and others found the girl and she lived. *Damn, damn, damn.*

Angrily, he gripped a sapling and stood still. He let the useless emotion drain sufficiently to continue down the path to the rainforest floor. There, he made his way toward his base camp. He had to regroup.

As he trod through the rainforest, his anger was replaced by a lost, empty feeling. He moved by instinct, realizing he was all in his head, oblivious to his surroundings, even to the urgency of impending retribution from Drake.

Damn. He had taken a freaking deer track. He quickly moved into the bush and continued, watching and listening, once again in control.

Or not.

His bungled assassination attempt left him conflicted. *Is this a sign I should cut my losses and leave? Have I pushed too far, overextended?* For the first time, he was unsure of the mission he had planned and executed flawlessly.

Up to this morning. With all the time in the world, top-notch hardware, a single unguarded target, not a bit of security. He felt humiliated, like that time when he was six years old, edging down crowded stairs during a school fire drill. He shoved the person in front of him, thinking it was the twerpy girl he didn't like, expecting to watch her tumble and cry.

But it was a boy, lean and mean. He punched Keller's nose and pushed *him* down the stairs. The girl had been there alright. She passed his crumpled form without a glance. *Yeah, humiliation.* That was what he felt.

Keller climbed the rock to his base camp, slipped through the ring of bushes, and sat on the hard rock. Humiliation was what he made *other* people feel. Experiencing the emotion felt foreign, unreasonable, impossible.

Was it bad to feel this way? Sure, the feeling felt nasty, but was it a truth, an experience he could fashion into a positive lesson? He shook his head. *Fuck no.* Humiliation had no place in his character. To dare with confidence, that had a place. To push and push hard until vanquishing the enemy, that had a place.

Well, good or bad, he did feel humiliation. His mind had weighed the morning's events and come up with humiliation. Like a stern father, telling him like it was – *you screwed up.* Okay, he felt humiliated. That was the only rational way to feel after such a failure. To feel happy was a lie. To reason that Murphy's Law took a turn at the wheel was a cop out.

He gazed at the perimeter of bushes, his concealment. Like his ghillie suit, like his jungle-green fatigues, they reflected his ideal of invisibility. While he remained invisible to his enemy, he was free to surveil, to kill, and to withdraw to fight another day. The bushes and camouflage represented strength.

Strength. That was what he owned. His humiliation would fade, buried beneath past and future victories. Beginning that afternoon, as planned. The explosion was, on one hand, too small because the girl survived. On the other hand, it was too large, because it dominated and did not simply distract. He stood, looked beyond his perimeter, and his eyes grew hard. He would carry out his mission this day.

Keller reached for water, but both jugs were empty. Time for refills. Chewing a piece of jerky, he descended from his rock and entered the rainforest. This time, his route was round about, and more than once he avoided an obvious break in brambles in favor of a circuitous alternative.

Only once did he retrace his steps from a former trek, the one he had taken the previous day, close to the creek and full of flat stones on which he trod, all but erasing his wraith-like presence. He approached the creek from the east bank, paused for five minutes under cover, rose and surveyed the surroundings, and ducked down for another minute.

Hearing all the usual animal sounds, he quickly stepped into the creek, here only up to his shins and five feet wide, and angled toward the fallen tree. He slipped under the leafy end of the tree, into his tented hide. He filled his empty canteen and his two jugs, and maneuvered out.

He scanned up and down the creek, clambered up the east bank and aimed back toward his base camp. He grasped the jugs in his left hand, his right hand free to draw his Afghan *peshkabz*. He touched the fearsome weapon and felt his usual confidence.

Keller ascended the boulder and stowed the jugs in the shade. He quickly downed field rations and guzzled water. Feeling the effects of a sleepless night, he napped on top of his sleeping bag. Hourly, through long habit, he awoke and checked the perimeter for intruders.

CHAPTER 38

Richard, George, Jimmy, and a fisherman named Pedro carried Sophie to Richard's bungalow. Color had returned to her face, and as the men scratched their heads trying to figure how to fit the stretcher through the door, Sophie half rose, rolled off the stretcher and stood.

She sketched a shaky grin. "I can make it from here."

The men stepped back, bemused, and Richard led the way inside. Jimmy hovered close. In the kitchen, she started to speak, but slow-motion collapsed into a chair.

Jimmy put a hand on her shoulder. "That's good, Sophie. Probably best to sit for a minute."

"Thanks, guys," she breathed.

Richard handed her a glass of water and she drank deeply. He stood aside, giving Jimmy space to gently poke and prod and ask questions. Sophie remained still, seemingly more spent by the ordeal than she had realized. She gave Richard a wan smile.

The fisherman approached Richard and quietly said, "I think Sophie will need a place for her store. We have that big stone warehouse. She can have half if she wants."

Richard hadn't thought that far ahead. "Great idea, Pedro. Are you sure you have the room?"

"Oh yeah. We'll move the boat and the nets and stuff. It'll be a good excuse for us to throw out all the junk that's been around for years. Do you think she'll like the idea?"

"She'll love it."

"Good. I've got to go now. We'll clear the place this morning and she can move in. We're happy to help. She's always friendly and kind to our wives and kids. She is a good person."

Richard extended his hand and they shook. "Thanks, Pedro. This will take away a lot of worry."

The fisherman smiled and departed.

After a few minutes, Jimmy stepped back, glanced at Richard and addressed Sophie. "You're bruised and I've dressed a couple of scrapes, Sophie. There are no burns, no broken bones or pulled tendons. But you need rest."

She gave him a look.

"I'm serious," he said. "A couple of hours sleep, at least."

Richard said, "It'll give the fishermen time to clear a space in their building."

She tilted her head in puzzlement and Richard said, "Pedro offered half the space for your store while you're waiting for repairs."

"My gosh! That's so generous of him."

"But first," Jimmy drawled.

She frowned at the men. "Do I get to at least wash my face?"

They nodded and she walked shakily into the bathroom.

Richard said, "I'll get her settled here. Shall we meet at your place?"

"Sure, we've got all day. But afterwards, um, Katie, you know." He blushed. "It's still cloak and dagger with her dad."

"Old school."

"Yeah. He'd keep her at home till she was forty if he had his way."

"I understand. Some of the folks on the island are pretty traditional. The idea of dating without a chaperone, all that. George is getting a little touchy about Jenny and she's only ten."

Jimmy chuckled. "Yeah, but Katie finds a way."

"Sounds good. I'll see you in a few minutes."

Jimmy left, and Sophie reappeared. She'd somehow slipped into the bedroom and had gotten into one of his t-shirts. He grinned. *Her hair's tousled and her eyes smudged, but damn she's gorgeous.* She kissed him and he took her hand and led her to the bed.

She looked up as he tucked her in. "I'll be *lonely*."

He tried to look stern and thought for a moment what a handful she must have been for her father. He kissed her and she smiled.

"Later," she said sleepily.

Almost immediately her breathing became deep and regular. On the way to Jimmy's house, he stopped at Pirate's Rest and asked for Asunción. She appeared, wiping her hands on a dish towel, and Richard said, "I want to ask your help for several hours."

"Of course, Richard. How is Sophie?"

"She's okay and she's sleeping at my place."

"So maybe I should be up there, just in case?"

"I was hoping. But can you get away?"

"Don't worry. Daniel can cook and wait tables. I will tell him and I will go up. He will be fine with that."

"He'll check on you?"

She smiled. "Yes, Richard. I will bar the doors and windows and stand guard of our precious Sophie. Where will you be?"

"At Jimmy's. Planning how to capture that man."

"That's even better." She patted his arm. "Now go. Sophie will be safe."

Richard handed her the key to the door, which was locked for the first time since Richard had moved into the place. Five minutes later, he arrived at Jimmy's house. His friend met him with a cold beer and motioned to the kitchen table. "You've been in the rainforest with Sophie, George, and alone, and you've seen that guy. What do you think?"

"He's trained and he's crafty. I told you about his tells and his booby trap, and you know about the two attacks on Sophie. I'll tell you this – it won't be a walk in the park."

"He'll be gunning for us."

"Yup. He's skilled and patient, and almost certainly has world-class weaponry."

"You think he's got a rifle?" Jimmy asked.

"Maybe, but the rainforest makes for close-quarter combat."

"Hand-to-hand?"

Richard nodded. "Pistols and knives."

"What's your plan?"

"I'm thinking we find him, cover him with pistols, and order him to surrender."

"Okay. How do we find him?"

"I've got that figured out. Every day or so, he fills his water jugs beneath a tree that lies half-across the creek."

"We wait for him?"

"Yeah," Richard said.

"What if he doesn't come? Or if he decides to burn down your house while you're away?"

"All that could happen. The thing is, we could play hide and seek with that guy for days and still not find him."

"Couldn't we starve him out?"

"It's an idea."

"But you think he'll come by this tree, right?"

"I do," Richard said. "The advantage in doing it that way is we're in control. We sneak in, hide where we can see the tree. He's got to show up."

"Then we follow him?"

"Right, until we can get at him from two angles. Then we call out. It's his choice from there."

They switched to black coffee and talked details, risk, and what-ifs.

Well past lunch, Richard stood. "I think that's about it, unless you have any other ideas."

"No, I'm fine. You'll loan me NVGs?"

"Yup. Do you have fresh ammo?"

"I'm fine."

"Is four o'clock tomorrow morning okay with you? Knock on your door?"

"That's fine." Jimmy extended his hand and they shook.

Back at his bungalow, Richard opened the door quietly with his spare key in case Sophie was asleep. He found a note on the kitchen table that read, "I'm up and better. Going to see about setting up store in fishermen's warehouse. Love, S."

He was tempted to go help her immediately but he was too keyed up. He opened his safe and pulled out his Glock, along with bore brushes, cleaning swabs, and luster cloth. He cleaned and oiled.

After an hour, still dwelling on a hundred details of the mission, he locked away his gear and walked to town.

144

CHAPTER 39

Late in the afternoon, Keller exited the valley. Fully refreshed from his nap, he acclimated himself to the sights and sounds of the dry forest, with its comparatively bald trees and desiccated bushes.

There was a different smell as well – more of dirt and sea salt than plants and flowers. He checked for loose strands on his ghillie suit, found one, and pocketed it for later disposal. He set a westward course, calm and collected, stepping carefully to avoid twigs that might snap and give him away.

Keller crossed the paved road and worked his way downward on the mountain. When woods gave way to fields of tall grass and occasional bushes, he crawled on his belly, pausing frequently to listen, keeping his head low. He spotted his target – Richard's bungalow – and course-corrected to the right. He continued until he was only fifty yards uphill of the place, then waited with the patience only a sniper knows.

When he looked at the remains of the store, those negative emotions again arose in his chest, and he resolutely channeled all thoughts to the mission at hand. Down in the town, he spotted a swarm of islanders hauling boxes and bags of stuff from where the store had been into one of the three large stone buildings. He even saw the girl, who looked no worse the wear.

Half an hour after he arrived, he heard a door close. It sounded like it was Drake's door, but the front of his cottage was blocked from view. It must have been his door, because a moment later, Drake appeared. He wore shorts, shirt, and sneakers, clothing not at all conducive to skulking around in the bush seeking immediate retribution. He walked down to town, crossed the street, and disappeared into the building that was apparently becoming the island's new general store.

Obviously, Drake was going to help the girl in the store. He'd be absent from the bungalow for at least an hour. Keller began the slow trek downward in the tall grass.

CHAPTER 40

As he paused to let his eyes adjust to the shadowed interior, Richard realized he'd never been inside the fishermen's warehouse. He knew it was one of three identical stone structures, the other two being The Pirate's Rest and the fire station. All were built during pirate days to house supplies to sell to renegades who would be hung if they dared call at St. Thomas. The ceiling was high, walls thick, and this afternoon the air smelled of fish, diesel oil, sawdust, and – what? – singed boxes.

His friend, Pedro, had been good to his word. Along the left side of the building stood a fishing boat, wooden frames festooned with nets, and a collection of chain, anchors, boat hooks, oars, and a dozen neatly-coiled lengths of rope. To the right, the floor had been swept clean to the original stone surface and, amid the sound of hammers and saws, shelving was being built.

Richard greeted George, who said, "We sort of took the day off. The fishermen had a stack of boards and told us we could use all we wanted for shelves."

"Looks good. There sure is enough room."

"Yep. The shelves will be pretty empty till the ferry arrives, but a few canned goods and things from the storeroom survived."

Richard found Sophie standing in a swirl of people sorting and stocking surviving goods. Through the front door a dozen people, many of them kids, gleefully hauled boxes and bags of goods and set them down, then returned for more. Apparently, among the kids, a game of tag was intertwined with carrying stuff.

He gave Sophie a peck on the cheek and squeezed her shoulder. "You didn't waste any time."

"I had to come – people need their supplies." She swept her arm around the scene. "And look! I think half the island is here!"

"Well, they do adore you, Sophie."

She laughed. "And I adore them. God help me, I'll treasure this moment for the rest of my life."

"It's like a family."

"Yes, it is. Oh, I wanted to take a final look at the old store and see if we'd forgotten anything."

He held her hand and they walked the hundred yards to the site. A sharp smell filled the air.

Sophie wrinkled her nose. "I guess it's plastic and rubber."

Jenny trotted over. "I think we got everything, Miss Sophie."

The other kids gathered, smiling up, and she said, "Thank you so much. You are all dears." She glanced at the boys. "Not you guys, of course. You are all so strong." They grinned and the little gang scampered noisily toward town.

Richard and Sophie stood with shoulders touching, gazing at the blackened remains. She pointed to the right. "That's where I set the booby trap. There were marbles all over the floor when I came in this morning, so he must have tripped the wire."

"Hopefully, tripping him as well."

"Yes."

She sighed and put her arm around his waist. "I don't see anything else worth saving. Richard, what can I do?"

"John didn't have insurance?"

"No, not a dime, and now I must build a new store. I can't impose on the fishermen forever. The business does make a profit, but my gosh."

"How long will it take to recover? How big a loan will you need?"

"It will be years." She mentioned a dollar amount.

"That's a lot of money. We can check with Mike and Anika. They may be able to recommend a bank to float a loan for the ruined supplies and a mortgage for the reconstruction. The island men, George's guys and a couple more, can provide labor. They won't charge much, if anything, you can be sure of that."

He turned and held her. *Enough talk for now.*

149

Afternoon had turned to dusk and no one was about. She snuggled in for a kiss and when their lips parted, she gave him a sultry look. He felt her hand exploring.

"Ooh, Richard, you're happy to see me."

He kissed her, hard and long, and was glad to see she surfaced short of breath, eyes wide.

"Let's go to dinner," he said.

"And?" Again, the sultry look.

"Yes, afterwards, at my place. I'll protect you from Keller and his explosions."

"I like the sound of that."

"Yup. We call it 'close-in security' in the Corps."

"That sounds very official. Hmm, how close?"

He hugged her again, smelling her hair, her scent. There was only the slightest whiff of smoke. They walked to The Pirate's Rest and chose a table on the deck, overlooking the harbor. Beers arrived and they both drank deeply.

Sophie smiled. "I guess kissing makes you really thirsty."

"I think so."

"Plus the heat and work of the day."

They touched bottles and drank again, not quite as deeply, and Richard admired her. *Pretty, spunky, and a fighter.* Also, in danger from Keller. His face must have shown the latter thought, because she put her bottle down and leaned forward.

"What?" she asked.

"I'm thinking about keeping that damned guy away from you. He's got a loose screw, Sophie." He shifted in his chair. "Also, I talked again with Mike, and we agreed that there's a link between those mysterious deaths I told you about and Keller and me."

"You?"

"Yes. The link is military service in Afghanistan. We were all there at the same time."

"Exact same time?"

He shrugged. "Some started earlier or ended later, but there was an overlap, say two weeks, when we were all there in the same combat zone."

She put her hand to her mouth. "My gosh, Richard. Do you think you're his real target? That he's after me only to hide his true intentions?"

"That's the idea."

"What's he after? He couldn't have a grudge against all three of you."

"It has to be something beyond a grudge. We don't know what."

She reached across the table and held his hand, her fingers chilly, whether from the cold beer or grim thoughts, he couldn't tell.

He said, "I finally figured out when I met him. It was during a period of about a week when he joined our unit. He went with us on a couple of patrols, kept to himself, asked a few questions. We talked only briefly."

"Why was he with your unit?"

"The best I can figure is he wanted to become familiar with the territory. Probably also wanted our safety in numbers, because he accompanied us a time or two and then branched off. We assumed he went on to conduct his own mission, then hiked back to camp solo or with his spotter if he had one. The last time I saw him was when he visited our post to debrief our commanding officer on his mission."

"What kind of mission?"

"I'd say he was a sniper. Snipers work alone, except for a spotter. Though, like I said, sometimes there wasn't a spotter." Richard thought back. "He was an Army officer. He made a point of saying good-bye to me, and he gave me that Afghan fighting knife you said looked exactly like his."

"You're going for him tomorrow?"

"Yes. Jimmy and I."

"I don't like thinking of that. He'll fight dirty."

"We will, too."

"God. I can't see how you do it."

"We don't have a choice."

The owner, Daniel Pearson, set two more beers on the table, and they ordered dinner. They remained quiet for a minute and changed the subject to the store inventory. Half-way through their second beers, they gave that up as too serious and branched into their evening plans.

After their meal, they were almost out the door when Asunción – Daniel's wife – rushed from the kitchen.

"Sophie, I have questions for you about Jenny's party. It will only take a minute, I promise."

"Okay," Sophie said, and to Richard, "I'll be right up."

Richard nodded, waved good-bye, and departed. He navigated the dark path, more by memory than vision in the nearly non-existent moonlight. He opened the front door, regretting he'd forgotten his flashlight and couldn't check the telltale.

He stepped inside.

Felt his way to a kerosene lantern and matches on the kitchen table.

Wondered what he was smelling. Gun-cleaning oil of course, but another scent. Oddly familiar.

Then everything went black.

CHAPTER 41

Richard awoke with cold water running down his face and a blurred view of a man holding an empty pot, and he blinked in the light of the kerosene lantern.

His lantern.

His kitchen.

What the hell?

Thin cord, like parachute line, bit into his wrists and ankles, securing him to a chair. He tasted bile.

The man set the pot on the table. "You've been out for less than five minutes, Drake. Nap time is over. Listen up and give me what I want. Understood?"

Richard blinked, furiously trying to clear the cobwebs in his brain. He glanced around the room, desperately searching for a way to turn the tables. The jalousies were all closed. He peered at Keller in his ghillie suit. The man who gave him the Afghan fighting knife. *Did he want that back?*

There was a faint rustle outside the front door. The knob turned a fraction, emitting a metallic chirp.

Sophie!

Richard coughed loudly. Hoped to hell Keller hadn't heard the noise. He was sitting further from the door, but close enough.

I have to warn her.

He looked Keller in the eye and said distinctly, hoping she could hear over the nighttime insects, "Hi Keller. It's been a while. Blow up anything lately?"

CHAPTER 42

Sophie scrambled up the path to Richard's house, chagrinned she'd chatted with Asunción far longer than necessary. She hoped Richard wouldn't be angry, and formed an apology as she turned the door knob to his bungalow.

She abruptly froze. From inside, she heard Richard's voice, loud and grim. Insect chatter masked his words, except for one – *Keller*.

She released her grip on the door knob.

Is Richard Keller's prisoner?

She placed her ear close to the door and covered the other ear with a shaking hand. Richard was goading Keller. The sniper responded without emotion, like a mechanical answering machine. She strained to understand the muffled conversation, to gather clues that might help.

What if Keller hears me? She resolved to run away the moment she heard footsteps. She would retreat up the mountain then toss a stone to one side to make him think she'd gone that way.

She shut her eyes and focused on the words. Had Keller come to negotiate? Or did he have other plans? She drew slow breaths, tried to calm her pounding heart.

Why weren't they talking?

No matter, she decided. *I need to find help. Now.*

She sped down the trail to town. Glanced at Pirate's Rest, saw a light around closed jalousies in the rear apartment where Daniel and Asunción lived. She nearly tripped twice and forced herself to slow down and mind the rocks in the path. She tore across the road and pounded on the front door.

No answer. She ran around back and knocked on the hurricane shutters to either side of the jalousies. Heard grumbles from inside.

"We're closed." Daniel's voice. Irritated.

Sophie shouted, "It's me. Richard's in trouble!"

The jalousie flapped open and she saw Daniel in his white boxers, hairy chest, tousled hair.

Asunción stood behind him, a hand on his shoulder. *¿Que pasa?*

Good, Sophie thought – *reverting to Spanish* – *she realizes this is serious.*

"You know that damned intruder?"

"*Sí.* I mean yes," Asunción said.

"He's taken Richard prisoner in his bungalow."

"*¡Díos mío!*

"How can we help?" Daniel asked.

"Where does Jimmy Franklin live?"

"Four houses to the left of Richard," Daniel said. "His place has bushes on either side of the door."

"*Sí,*" Asunción added. "His girlfriend planted them."

"Which path is fastest?" Sophie asked.

"Turn left from Pirate's Rest. Fifty yards after the path to Richard's, turn uphill at the big rock. Pass a house or two, then Jimmy's is on the left. The only one with bushes. I'll come with you."

"No," Sophie said, knowing Daniel would soon run out of breath and delay her. "Do you have a flashlight?"

"Here, *tome,*" Asunción said, pushing a penlight through the louvers. "It is small but *muy* powerful."

Sophie grasped the light. "Thanks."

Out front, she turned and jogged, playing the light to the uphill side of the road, sighting the first path and casting a worried glance up toward Richard's bungalow, then continuing.

The big rock was painted white, easy to see in the beam of the penlight. She scampered up the trail, beam down to tell her were to place her feet. Passed one house. Another.

Two bushes, a door between. All was dark.

Too bad, Jimmy. Time to wake up.

She pounded on the door. No answer. She leaned close and heard vague clattering inside. She pounded again.

And again.

"Okay, okay, I'm coming. Who's hurt? Where are they?"

Sophie felt a glimmer of hope. That was Jimmy's voice, and he seemed more resigned than angry. No doubt he was accustomed to being awakened in the middle of the night.

He opened the door a crack. More white boxers, male chest.

"What?!" he asked, finger-combing hair out of his eyes.

"Who is it?" came a female voice behind him.

Jimmy frowned. Shook his head, gestured with his free hand. Silence behind him. "Hi Sophie. Sorry about my – er – *pajamas.*"

"Richard is being held prisoner in his kitchen by Keller."

Jimmy's frown deepened. "Come inside. I'll be a minute. You know Katie."

"Hi Sophie."

"Hi Katie. Um. Sorry to disturb you. I – er – didn't – "

Katie, blushed, then she put her hand to her mouth and gasped, "Wait! Did you say Richard is in trouble?"

"Yes. That awful man has him."

"Jimmy!"

"Be right there, sweetie. Getting dressed. Where are my jungle boots?"

Katie giggled, gave Sophie a sideways look, and disappeared into the other room. Her voice drifted out. "Um, they're under the bed, honey, right next to your Randall knife."

Jimmy growled, "Katie."

"Sorry," she said, "I didn't want you to leave tonight. I figured if the boots and knife were tucked away, well, you know."

"Katie, if I weren't in such a hurry, I'd – "

Giggles from the other room, then Katie said, "Here are your boots and socks. Hmm, here's your Randall. You need your pistol?"

"Thanks, thanks, yup, pistol. Top drawer. Extra clips too. Flashlight."

"Got 'em. You take care."

Jimmy appeared, dressed in jungle fatigues. Scowled at the front door. He kissed Katie good-bye and to Sophie he said, "Let's get that son of a bitch."

Sophie opened the door and ran down the path, hearing Jimmy right behind her. At the road, she saw Daniel, who waved.

At the turning up to Richard's bungalow, Jimmy put his hand on her arm and she stopped. He glanced at the fishermen's warehouse. "I need something." He strode across the street.

Sophie caught up with him, opened the small 'person' door in one of the looming main doors, and led the way into the dark and musty space. "Should I light a lantern?"

"No." He shined his light away from the store and its aisles of goods, the beam illuminating a boat, nets, and vaguely-shaped mystery piles. He maneuvered toward one of the mystery piles. "Can you find matches and a can of lighter fluid?"

"Sure." Sophie found both, located on a high shelf, away from little-kid fingers. *What is he up to?* She forced herself not to hurry him along, realized he had a plan.

Jimmy returned, grasping a long stick and a handful of rags reeking of oil. He took the lighter fluid and matches from her and stuffed them into his pants pockets. "Let's go."

Outside, at the start of the path to Richard's bungalow, he switched off his flashlight and whispered, "No lights from here on. No talking. If you want to say something, touch my shoulder, and I'll do the same with you. Then we get close and whisper, but make it quiet and short. Okay?"

She nodded, surprised she could make out his silhouette, if only vaguely, but enough to see him nod as well.

Jimmy whispered, "Um, one other thing. Katie's dad and mom think she's in bed in her room."

Sophie squeezed his arm. "Don't worry."

Jimmy led the way, Sophie a couple of feet behind. The bungalow materialized above them, then they were there, ten feet from the door. Jimmy made a 'hold it here' gesture.

She nodded and he crept forward, one step at a time, until he reached the bungalow. He moved like a shadow around to the right, and peeked through a gap between closed jalousie louvers.

After five minutes, he returned and guided Sophie twenty feet back down the path. He whispered into her ear, "Richard is tied to a chair in the kitchen. Keller is after information but Richard is not talking. Keller is threatening him."

"My God."

"Yes. We've got to hurry. Sophie, there's something I need you to do."

CHAPTER 43

Remaining motionless, Richard explored the knots at his wrists. All were tight, but perhaps not too tight. From the smooth feel and small diameter of the line, he was almost certain it was US military parachute cord, too strong to break. However, its braided outer sheath was Nylon, which was slippery. Not enough to make knots ineffective but helpful in working them loose.

He concentrated on the most accessible knot, bothering it with his fingernails. Expending minimum force, he kept his arm tendons from rising and alerting Keller.

The sniper tilted his head a fraction, as if weighing how to force Richard to talk. At length, he pushed aside a fold in his ghillie suit and displayed the bone handle of his *peshkabz*. Richard gazed straight ahead, ignoring the implicit threat.

Earlier, Richard had verbally pushed Keller because he wanted to distract him from the sound of the jiggling doorknob. Those sounds had stopped several minutes ago. Sophie must have gone for help. That hurdle was successfully jumped – Sophie was safe. Now his goal was to gain time for help to arrive.

Richard decided to appear calm and seek an opening for negotiation. He glanced at the man, who looked furious, judging from the taut muscles around his eyes and mouth. A kitchen clock ticked as minutes passed. At first, the interlude appeared to soften Keller's features, but then the man's jaw muscles bunched, adding to Richard's feeling of impending aggression.

He worked desperately at the knot but it was small and remained tight. Richard's only option was to divert Keller from upping the ante. The last thing he wanted was for him to begin slicing and dicing with the *peshkabz*. That was a one-way trip.

Keeping his tone conversational, Richard said, "You're the man who's been following Sophie."

"Sophie? That's her name?"

"Yes, it is. You chased her from the valley. Was she bothering you? Trespassing?"

"I was camping out. Alone. I didn't like her intruding."

"You're Tim Keller."

Keller rose from the chair, stepped belligerently toward Richard, then held himself in check. "Yes, I'm Keller."

"We went on a couple of patrols together, talked a few times."

"That's right."

"I don't remember problems between us. And you haven't even met Sophie. Why attack her? Has someone hired you? If so, they might have lied to you. She's innocent."

Keller shook his head, a mocking sadness in his reply. "Innocent? I wouldn't care if she were Mother Teresa. She was an instrument of tactics, a diversion."

Which fit Richard's tentative conclusions and confirmed that he, Richard, was Keller's target. "Okay, Tim, that makes sense. A diversion. Always a good tactic to keep your adversary off balance. What do you want with me?"

"Ah, now we get to it. I need you to give me the combination to your safe."

"But why? Are you after a few pistols?"

"Wrong response." Keller stepped close and backhanded Richard.

Richard turned with the blow, which softened the impact, but he still saw stars.

"The combo," Keller growled. "I'll take it from there. I may even let you live."

Richard needed time. Taking a risk of enraging Keller, he asked, "Unlike the others?"

"Others?" He held Richard's gaze for a moment and appeared to make a decision. "Yes. The others died. They knew me. They knew too much. The combo, Richard."

"You lied. Just now, you lied."

"About letting you live? Yes. I like you, but you are a link to me, just like the others."

Richard's sweaty fingers continued to bother the knot.

Keller fisted his right hand and leaned forward, his expression murderous.

Richard tightened his abs.

I've run out of time.

CHAPTER 44

Sophie and Jimmy stood together on the path. He appeared suddenly different from the peaceful man known as 'doc,' who always had time to toss a ball with the kids or chat with the women or share a beer with the men. This man faced her with eyes black and dangerous. Normally – always – his eyes were inviting, even charming, making a listener believe they were the most important person in his world.

Not now, not as he grasped her shoulders and stared, inches from her, those eyes boring into her, compelling her to listen, to obey. Because at that moment he made *himself* the most important person in *her* world.

"Okay," she said, feeling like a pinned butterfly, "tell me how I can help."

"Go down and ring the alarm bell at the fire station. That'll wake the volunteers and they'll come running. Daniel and others will show up as well. Tell them to pretend there's a fire next door to Richard's place. Tell them to make lots of noise, like the fire is out of control and spreading, heading for the neighboring houses."

"Okay, Jimmy."

"Keller will hear men shouting orders and he'll see the fire engine." Jimmy brandished the oily rags. "He'll smell the fire."

"What will you do?"

"Chase that damned man away. Now go. Be quick."

She sprinted down the path, ran directly to the fire station and rang the big brass bell. Men appeared on the run and disappeared into the fire station. Several returned, donning boots and fire outfits.

A man asked, "Where is it?"

Others gathered around. Daniel approached and said, "I have runners out to all the houses."

She shook her head, remembering the urgency in Jimmy's eyes. "We can't wait for them." To the firemen she said, "The intruder on the island has Richard tied up in his house. Jimmy has a plan and needs your help. Starting now, you have to act as if there's a fire in the house next to Richard's. Put on a good show."

A few nods. Many blank stares.

She forced herself to remain calm and appear sure of herself. She looked from person to person, pausing on each for a split second, then onward. "Your noise – and the Jeep's as well – *will* be loud and *will* stay that way for as long as it takes to drive the guy out into the open and away from Richard."

"But there is no fire."

"Keller can't see that! Don't you understand? We make him believe that the house next door is an inferno, threatening to burn down Richard's house as well."

Plenty of nods now. Four men jumped into the fire engine. Sophie sprinted up the path, aware of others right behind. She stopped below Richard's bungalow.

The fire truck clawed uphill with its four-wheel drive and stopped fifty feet to the left. The driver gunned the engine, three men unwound the hose. There were loud shouts and orders. Men clanged shovels at the ground as if forming a fire break.

The door of the next-door house opened and a man appeared in shorts and t-shirt. "What's going on?"

A firemen patted his shoulder. "No worries. We're causing a riot to rescue Richard. That damned stranger is in there holding him prisoner."

The man nodded, still half-asleep. The racket continued for five minutes, then came the sharp crack of a shot. Mouths opened in surprise, heads glanced left and right, trying to locate the source.

Another shot, from the back of Richard's house.

A third.

Then only cicadas and the idling fire truck.

CHAPTER 45

Keller massaged his hands, sore from striking the stubborn man seated in front of him. Blood streamed from Drake's nose and mouth. Bruises on his jaw and gut were beginning to color.

He kicked the man's chair in frustration. So near, and this shit-for-brains idiot decided to play hero. Keller stepped back and took a breath. *Life is too short for this crap.* He had to get the job done and leave the freaking island.

What to do? Ah, yes. In three steps, he was at the kitchen counter, lined with drawers, which he jerked open and dropped onto the floor in a clanging mess of spoons, forks, knives, and spatulas. He examined the mix with a seasoned eye. *Yes, the ice pick. Works every time.*

He heard new sounds outside – shouts, a ringing bell. The same bell as when he'd blown up and burned the store. *Oh yeah, the fire alarm.*

Keller cracked open a jalousie louver. Luckily, the single lantern would barely show in case they got nosy, though it was bright enough to screw up his night vision. Should he blow it out? *Not yet. See what's going on, then decide.*

Men climbed the hill and moved to the right, gestured and called to one another. *Damn, this looks serious.* He caught words – 'fire,' 'next to Richard's.'

A tendril of smoke curled through the jalousies. He sniffed. *I can't believe this shit!* He had been on the mountain a half dozen nights and nothing had happened. The whole town went to sleep by nine o'clock. The damned insects were the only things making noise. *Now, this night, there's a fire?'*

The smoke increased, borne on a draft, even though the jalousies on the other side of the house were closed. Yeah, he'd noticed that at night, some houses closed the shutters as well, but not the Marine.

Smoke collected in a light haze. He sniffed and sensed oil. Maybe a lantern tipped over next door and started the blaze. He debated whether to check the other windows, get a look at the place next door, and figure his chances of the fire fighters getting the fire under control.

A loud engine joined the racket and he peered out, saw a Jeep with a big tank on the back. Oh yeah, he'd seen that at the store. Their version of a fire truck. Pathetic. Guys climbed out, all suited up, unreeled a hose and moved out of his range of vision to the other house.

As minutes ticked by the noise increased, like they were losing the battle. Someone pounded on the door. A man yelled, "Richard! Richard!"

Drake turned toward the door, then looked at Keller, eyebrows raised in question.

"Don't make a sound," Keller growled. "You're not here."

"They know I am," he said very quietly. "I had dinner at Pirate's Rest and walked home. The owner's wife saw me."

Keller stared at the door. Thankfully, the pounding stopped. "Well, that guy sure didn't see you. He gave up. Figured this place is empty."

"But that's not the problem, Keller. The problem is the burning house next door. This one's next. Can't you feel the heat?"

"No, I *cannot* feel the heat, damn it!"

"You saw what happened to the store. Went up in a flash."

"That was the explosion, you dumb ass!" He turned back to the jalousie. Smoke poured through. He coughed. So did Richard. Keller thought, *If they could just do their freaking job and put out the fire.*

"It's getting worse," Richard said. "They arrived too late. They'll be running out of water any second."

Again, the pounding at the door, insistent, followed by a new voice. "Richard, I'm coming in. Don't shoot, man!"

Keller shoved Richard hard, tipping him onto the floor. "Sleep tight, asshole."

He sprinted out the back door, never looking back. He had no time for stealth, no need either, in all the confusion. Behind him, the front door splintered and slammed against the wall. *Good, he'll be delayed, saving Drake.*

Keller trotted up the hill, completely pissed at the universe.

Then a shot sounded. *What the hell?*

He poured on the steam, zig-zagged right and left, even though the shooter's visibility was nil. *Unless he wore NGVs.*

Crap. Keller gulped air and pumped his legs.

CHAPTER 46

Richard lay on the floor, bound to the chair. Keller had gone, his footsteps fading out back. Jimmy had broken through the front door and rushed through the kitchen to the back yard. Thunderous shots sounded, and Richard prayed that Jimmy was shooting at Keller and not the other way around.

A man loomed above him, wearing jungle fatigues, not a ghillie suit, and Richard let loose a pent-up breath. He looked up at a smiling Jimmy Franklin.

Jimmy holstered his pistol and sliced through Richard's bonds. He declared, "That boy's gone running! He looked like some kind of Jumbee with that baggy camo suit flapping in the dark. I wish we had a couple more combats vets on the island, waiting for that bastard out back. We could've netted him and been done."

Richard stood and gave his friend a hug. "No worries, Jimmy. You and I will get him real soon. Thanks, bud. You saved my bacon this time."

Jimmy looked Richard up and down. "Always a pleasure. You okay? Anything broken?"

"I'm fine."

"Alright. Your lady is outside. Probably wondering about the pistol shots."

Richard strode through the shattered front door, into the night air. When the guys realized they were looking at a free Richard Drake, they danced a jig, whooped and hollered.

Sophie arrived in a blur and hugged and kissed him. Still holding tight, she backed off only enough to see his face, the blood, and hints of bruising, visible in the headlights of the Jeep.

"Richard – what has that awful man done to you?"

"Nothing much." He made eye contact with the others, now crowding around. "But you all came right on time. He was poking around my kitchen drawers, looking for a torture tool I believe. The fact is, you fire fighters saved me. You, and these two."

He hugged Sophie with one arm, and Jimmy with the other. "That man was going to steal something from my safe – he never did say what – and then was going to kill me because I was a witness. Thank you, all. I love you!"

More cheering, a couple of gentle pats on the back, then the fire fighters trudged down toward the fire station, followed by their fire engine. Sophie had disappeared inside Richard's bungalow with Jimmy, and by the time Richard said his final good-byes, they were waiting at the door.

Sophie handed him a cold beer. Jimmy patted a chair next to the kitchen table. He spread out meds, bandages, and a cold pack.

Richard placed the cold pack against his right jaw. "Is all this necessary?"

"The beer or the ice?" Sophie asked, voice teasing but eyes concerned.

"All those bandages."

"We'll see," Jimmy said. "I need to take a close look."

Richard winced as his friend touched the tender spots, and after a minute rose and looked him in the eye.

Jimmy said, "You'll need to rest for a couple days. Fortunately, there's no damage to your organs, no cracked ribs, best I can tell. Got some bruises on your face."

Richard frowned. "Rest for a couple days?"

Jimmy took a long swig of beer. "Just joking. You're approved for action."

Richard got up and clapped him on the shoulder. "No one would ever guess you were a combat medic, your bedside manner is so tender."

"Doin' my job."

"You two are terrible," Sophie said, trying to scowl, but dissolving into tears. She hugged them both. "God, I love you. Especially this big guy here, but you too, Jimmy. I'd die if anything happened to either of you."

They opened fresh beers and stood still for a minute. Richard excused himself, went into his bedroom and opened the safe. He withdrew two sets of night vision goggles, his Glock, and spare ammo, then locked the safe. He donned jungle combat fatigues and boots, grabbed a rain parka, and returned to the kitchen, laying his gear and his daypack on the table. He packed the gear, along with rations for a day, and filled his canteen.

"We've gotta go, Sophie."

She dabbed her eyes. "I know. And I know you'll find him. Just the same as when you beat Cliff – the two of you. You won't give up and you will win."

Richard gave her a hug, then Jimmy hugged her as well, his being brotherly, Richard's amorous.

"You'll be fine here," Richard said to Sophie. "I'll put the front door back and jam it tight with a chair, just to be sure."

She nodded.

Richard and Jimmy walked to Jimmy's house to round up the rest of his gear. As they stepped inside, Richard sniffed the air.

"Is that perfume?"

Jimmy cleared his throat as he lit a kerosene lantern. "Katie came by earlier."

Richard smiled to himself, remembering Jimmy telling him earlier that he had evening plans. Jimmy and Katie had been sweet on each other for almost a year. Everyone agreed things were getting mighty serious.

Jimmy looked questioningly at his medic satchel and Richard shook his head. "Too bulky for running through the bush."

Jimmy nodded, rifled through a drawer, pulled out a compact field medical kit, and stuffed it into his daypack.

Richard blew out the lantern and followed his friend into the night.

CHAPTER 47

Keller worked his way through the bush toward the valley, thinking through the events of the previous hour. He concluded that the shots were for show, because he'd been well out of pistol range.

But there was something else.

He reviewed those final minutes in Drake's house. The fire fighters, shouting and carrying on like they'd never seen a fire before. The Jeep with its four-wheel drive, straining to lug its tank of water up the steep mountain. The smoke, with its mix of smells.

What was it?

Were those scumbags tricking me? Maybe, but how? There *was* a fire. He'd heard the urgency of the fire fighters with their gear, heard and saw the Jeep, smelled the smoke.

The smoke, the smoke. Why did it smell like it came from an engine repair shop?

He balled his fists. *Damn them!* They'd dipped rags in diesel oil and lit them, poked them at the jalousies, and let that smoke blow into the kitchen.

He felt his face flush with rage. There was no freaking fire except on the end of a freaking stick.

He pounded his fist into his other hand. Swore. Toyed with the idea of going right back there and – but he knew it was too late. Whoever shot at him was still there. Hell, Richard had armed up by now and was itching to fight.

Keller decided he'd better check on the Zodiac, just to be sure. He might need to make a quick exit and didn't want to get delayed with mechanical problems or an air leak caused by an animal chewing holes in the hull. He headed north, toward the shoreline.

At length, he felt a cool breeze on his face and spotted the inky-dark Atlantic ahead. He turned east, and after ten minutes stopped at the familiar beach. Beneath a cover of palm fronds, the Zodiac appeared exactly as he'd left it.

He inflated the boat, confirmed there were no leaks, then dug a hole in the ground back aft, where the outboard motor would extend below the hull. He hefted the outboard into place and cranked it up. It fired on the first pull, smooth and powerful. He shut it down.

Keller poked around, found his gear and food stashes. He left the gear but set the food in the Zodiac. He covered the boat and motor with palm fronds. Satisfied all was well, he sat back and guzzled the remaining water from his canteen.

On the return to base camp he followed deer tracks, which quickened his journey by avoiding detours around closely-packed bushes. It was getting late and he needed sleep for the coming day. He entered the valley from the north entrance, made his way down, then crossed the creek to his base camp.

Immediately, he took out his night vision goggles and scanned the perimeter. All clear. He set the NGVs down and stretched out on his sleeping bag. He tossed and turned for an hour, then slept fitfully, one ear open, pistol at his side.

CHAPTER 48

Certain that Keller had withdrawn to his lair, Richard hiked up the road with Jimmy, aiming for the valley and impatient for action. As he climbed, he felt the weight of the *peshkabz* knife and scabbard in his right boot – his backup.

He murmured, "We should stop at George's and let him know what we're doing."

"He'll be sleeping,"

"Right. We'll approach slowly. Anyway, the dogs will warn him."

Ten minutes later, the Coxon houses came into view, bathed in a ghostly light from the sliver of moon. Trees swayed gently in the sea breeze. Dogs started barking as soon as they entered the broad front lawn, and rushed toward them in a pack. Richard stood still and Jimmy followed suit.

When the dogs got close enough to sniff Richard's scent, growls and bared teeth changed to wagging tails. They bumped against the men's legs and paused for head scratches and pats on their sides, then bounded back to the main house.

Someone lit a lantern inside, showing yellow through the jalousies. When they reached the stairs, George emerged, bare footed, in khaki shorts and untucked t-shirt, carrying a lantern. "Hi, Richard. Jimmy. Come on up. I heard the fire bell. Everything okay?"

The three of them sat on the porch with the lantern on a table, the dogs snoozing at their feet.

Richard said, "Keller bushwhacked me in my place. Sophie called Jimmy, and between them and the fire fighters and their noisy Jeep, made Keller think the house next door was a raging inferno. He hightailed it out. We figure he's back in valley."

"Expecting you to follow?"

"Yeah, first thing tomorrow."

George peered at Richard. "Looks like you got into a fight, from those bruises."

"Keller wanted the combination to my arms safe and I wouldn't tell him. I was trying to buy time until Sophie brought help."

"What did he want?"

"He never said, but I suspect it was the *peshkabz* he gave me when he was leaving Afghanistan."

"You seem to have gotten his attention at least."

"Yeah, and I confirmed he's after me, not Sophie. She was a distraction."

"Hell of an ass to pick on an innocent person like that. He must've had other options."

"Maybe, but his next step could have been to kidnap her as a way to get that combination."

"So you're going after him now?"

"That's right. We'll sneak into the valley and lay for him. I believe he'll be up and ready as soon as he can see his way around. He'll set an ambush. If he kills me, then he'll discover that he no longer needs to get inside my safe. At least, if he *is* after the *peshkabz*." Richard pulled up the cuff of his right trouser leg and exposed the hilt of the knife.

George nodded.

Richard said, "He probably expects I won't come alone. For sure, he saw you and Jimmy when we checked out the valley, and he'll look for one or both of you to be with me."

"He's a dangerous man and probably well-armed."

"Yes. I'm sure he packs knife and pistol, maybe grenades as well. Plus, he might have set a couple of nasty booby traps."

"I'm sure Sophie told you to be careful."

"Yeah, we plan to move slow and easy, make the capture, and bring him in."

"Alright," George said. "Anything I can do to help?"

"A couple of things. Close up your houses with the hurricane shutters, barred from the inside. Everyone stays in the main house. If Jimmy or I don't show up by ten o'clock tomorrow morning, notify Graham and ask for armed help."

"I'll do that."

"Good. Brief him. Tell him to expect Keller to be on his way over there or to one of the British islands. He's got a Zodiac stashed on the north shore. Also, one other thing." Richard handed George a folded piece of paper. "That's a note to Sophie. If I don't come back, I want her to have my bungalow."

"Jeeze," George whispered, taking the note and putting it in his shirt pocket.

Richard and Jimmy exchanged a look. Jimmy's eyes were all business, and he knew his were as well.

"Just a precaution," Richard said, his voice casual, but feeling a heavy lump in his throat. He rose and the others did as well. Richard and Jimmy shook hands with George.

Back in the bush and approaching the valley, Richard pulled out two sets of night vision goggles, gave one to Jimmy, and donned the other. He scanned the forest, which looked as if someone had switched on a green light. They continued along a deer track, and at the valley rim they paused, took swigs from canteens, and began the steep descent.

Beneath the canopy, visibility was good with the NGVs. The rain had turned into a steady downpour, pattering on the canopy and flowing through. They both donned ponchos.

Richard whispered, "When we reach the valley floor, we'll leave the deer track. There's always a chance Keller is out there ready to ambush us, though I'm hoping he's at his base camp, sleeping."

"Okay."

"I'm thinking we aim for that place I was telling you about where Keller gets his water."

"The tree that's lying over the creek bank?"

"That's it. We'll remain on the west side, to prevent him from running into us. We'll be close to the bank, hidden, but with a view of the tree. He has to wade into the creek to enter through the tree branches to where he stores his water bottles. As soon as he disappears, you'll cross the creek and cover a possible rear exit from the tree. I'll remain at our observation site. We'll have him boxed in."

"You think he'll surrender?"

"I don't know. He's unpredictable. We've got to be ready for him to come out shooting."

"Rules of engagement – shoot to kill?"

"Absolutely."

They reached the valley floor and left the deer track as planned, Richard leading the way, glancing from time to time at a field compass for bearing.

When he heard the babbling creek, he stopped, waited for Jimmy to catch up, and whispered, "We'll continue to the bank of the creek. Keep an eye peeled toward the other side for the fallen tree."

Jimmy nodded. Richard crept forward, knowing he was on Keller's home ground. He became especially alert to any change in the jungle sounds, and for that ticklish feeling that someone was watching.

Richard sensed no changes, no tickling, but he stopped cold at the edge of a small clearing. Why, he couldn't say. He gestured for Jimmy to back up a pace, then stood with his hands on his hips, scanning leaves, air plants, orchids, vines, and towering trees. He saw no straight lines that indicated a trip wire, no oddly-angled branches that indicated pent up energy to be released and smash into the unwary.

He lowered his search pattern to the height of a man and scanned the edge of the clearing. *Hmm, kill zone.* All the surrounding bushes were dense and prickly. There was only one other exit, at the opposite side, as if guiding the traveler across and out. He found that both exits were partially overgrown, forcing a person to push through.

Finally, he searched the forest floor – leaves twigs, small branches. He also found branches a little larger lying on the floor, some bare, others with leaves attached. A pattern emerged – half the branches lay one way, the other half at ninety degrees.

Intertwined among the branches were vines. He reached out, careful not to step inward, toward the center of the clearing. He grasped a vine and pulled it to himself. Examined both ends. He'd expect the ends to be rotten. Otherwise, the vine would not have fallen. One end was blackened and mushy to the touch. But the other had been cleanly cut. He inspected several branches and found all were cleanly cut.

He turned to Jimmy and motioned for him to help pull away enough of the foliage to see through to what he expected to find. They removed only a half dozen leafy branches, and saw below them a three-foot deep pit. Set on the bottom were rows of sharpened stakes, pointing upward. *Punji sticks*. This was a man trap.

Jimmy's eyes widened and he whispered, "You just saved us from a world of hurt."

They backtracked out of the clearing and continued north along the creek. After five minutes, Richard pointed at the familiar shape of a tree, slanted between shore and creek. Jimmy nodded in understanding and Richard led the way until just downstream of the tree, with a full view of the entrance Keller used to get inside the branches.

They hid within a clump of spiky bushes, out of sight, but with a clear view of the tree and its immediate surroundings. Richard took off his daypack. Crossed his legs and adjusted his poncho to protect pack and legs. "I'll take the first watch if you'd like."

In under a minute, Jimmy was curled up on the ground, wrapped in his poncho, using his daypack as a pillow, his pistol in hand, still wearing the night vision goggles.

Richard settled in for a boring few hours. The environment was completely different from that in Afghanistan, but the waiting and the tension were exactly the same.

CHAPTER 49

After Richard and Jimmy disappeared into the night, the bungalow felt deserted. No – worse than deserted. The place felt violated by that awful man.

Sophie surveyed the kitchen. Not a mark remained of Keller's presence. Yet she cringed when she looked at the chair where Richard had been bound and tortured. She wiped away tears and retreated to the bedroom.

She was in no mood to return to the kitchen, and she wasn't hungry anyway. She decided to call it a day. Or a night, really. It was now nearly midnight. She had no jammies with her, so she pulled out a pair of Richard's boxers and a t-shirt. They were clean and cool and reminded her of him. When she curled up in bed she discovered his scent on the pillow. That helped.

Still, she tossed and turned for an hour. The problem was, she needed *him*, to wrap her arms around and kiss, and to feel his presence. Most of all, to know he was safe.

Sleep came, but with creepy dreams of being chased through a deep jungle, naked of course.

Pursued by Keller.

        *   *   *

Soon after sunrise, Sophie traced her way down the path from the bungalow to town. Her mind was full of worry for Richard. He was in danger. Jimmy, too. They hunted a violent killer. Keller was trained, combat hardened, and aggressive. He'd fight and he'd shoot to kill.

She banished that train of thought. Richard and Jimmy had saved her once, against killers at least as nasty and dangerous as Keller. They were the A-team in this fight. They would win. That was the belief she must hold onto.

Sophie entered the fishermen's building. The large doors were wide open. Two men sat in the morning sun near the front. She watched them mend nets with weathered hands and quick fingers.

"Good morning," she said. "You're not out fishing today?"

"No," one said, looking up and grinning. "We drew the short straws, so today we mend everyone's nets. The others fish, and they split their profits with us."

"That sounds fair."

"We'd rather be at sea," said the other man. "We go in all sorts of weather. Today, the rain moved to its usual place over to the east end, and where we fish there is blue sky and gentle wind."

"But maybe you can have a beer with lunch, and when you go home, your wives won't say you smell like fish."

The men laughed, still mending as they talked. "You see the bright side, Sophie."

She continued to the other half of the building. Cruising the aisles, she checked the salvaged items arranged on the shelves and looked forward to filling in the blank spots with what the ferry would bring.

Her thoughts returned to Richard. Where was he now? In the valley, probably well off any of the established deer tracks. Judging from the clouds, he and Jimmy were getting rained on.

At the sound of footsteps, she looked up, surprised that someone would be there so early. It was Jimmy's girlfriend.

Sophie smiled. "Hi, Katie."

Black shadows underscored her eyes. "Hi, Sophie. I didn't come to buy anything. I needed to see you. You know how it is for your guy to be in danger. It's new to me and very scary."

They hugged and Sophie felt they needed each other. True, Katie was five years her junior and born and raised on normally-safe St. Mark. But Sophie was scared too, even though she'd faced danger before.

Katie asked, "When will they come back?"

"By evening, I think. Richard's explored the valley a couple of times, including with George, who goes there to cut wood for his boats and really knows the place. He and Jimmy will find Keller for sure."

"You sound confident."

Sophie gave her another hug. "I know our guys are very good at this sort of thing. We don't see their military side too often, and we start to think of only their smiles and jokes. But I saw the other side of Jimmy last night. He's a fighter, Katie, and so is Richard. I'm sure you've heard of how they beat those people who tried to harm me last year."

"Yes, they made a scary job sound easy." She looked around the store, over at the fishermen, and back at Sophie. "I wish I was with him. I know that sounds silly, but that's how I feel."

"Yeah, me too, but we've got to let them do this."

"Sophie, I have an idea. Why don't we go to the Coxons' house? At least we'd be closer to our guys. It would feel like we're doing *something*."

Sophie looked at her friend, a person she knew through her visits to the store and a couple of double dates with Richard and Jimmy. She was bright and normally happy, the perfect personality for her work, which was teaching the island kids from first to fifth grade.

She had told stories of her teaching experience, and Sophie noticed that Katie always seemed to have a way of making bad situations better. One day, after an hour of arithmetic that seemed to baffle and frustrate Jenny and her gang, she took everyone to the blow hole to unwind. They romped and laughed, and actually settled down and – one by one – caught on to long division.

"What?" Katie asked. "What are you thinking?"

"About that time you used the blow hole to teach math. And I like your idea. First, let's check with George and make sure it's okay."

Sophie and Katie walked together, holding hands most of the way to the boatyard, past sleepy dogs. The sky was bright blue, the dew gone.

Oddly, there were no sounds of saws and hammers. They approached the open-air assembly area where the small version of a Tortola sloop lay across saw horses, receiving final coats of paint

179

on her gracefully curved hull. Sophie waved to the half dozen men sitting in a semicircle, faces bronzed from working in the sun.

"Have you heard anything?" one asked, his face in shadow. He stood, and Sophie recognized Michael.

"No. Oh, hi, Michael. No, we haven't heard anything. Is your dad here? We had a question for him."

"No, Miss Sophie. He's at home with Mom and Jenny. They've shuttered the house like for a hurricane. Mr. Richard said to hold tight till he and Jimmy caught the stranger. Dad said for me to come to the boatyard today, and run back home if Mr. Richard and Mr. Jimmy came back here directly."

Sophie looked at the men, the tools lying here and there. One of the men cleared his throat and glanced at Michael.

Michael exchanged a look with the man, running his gaze over the others. "Actually, Miss Sophie, all we're doing is talking about what's going on in the valley. Wishing we could help." He shared a smirk with the men. "But we admit we'd just get in the way if they'd taken us along."

Nods by the other men.

"Well," Sophie said, "Katie and I were thinking we might go on out to your folks' place. You know, maybe help while we all waited for the guys to return. Then we could be there for them in case, well, if they needed anything."

Michael nodded slowly. Like his dad, he was a good listener, and he paused before talking, another habit his dad possessed. Finally, looking more mature than his fourteen years, he addressed the men, his voice relaxed.

"Guys, maybe we should forget about trying to work today. Wives and families will be thinking of nothing else, and we can show support by being with them."

The men, whose ages ran from twenties to sixties, took that on board with solemn looks and murmured their agreement. *My gosh*, Sophie thought. *He's earned their respect, that's for sure. The apple didn't fall far from the tree.*

Everyone began picking up tools, putting caps on paint cans, and cleaning brushes. One said, "We'll see you bright and early tomorrow, Michael."

"Sounds good," Michael said. "The ladies and I will be walking to our place. Mr. Richard said he and Mr. Jimmy will stop there when they're done. I'll come to town as soon as we know what happened, and spread the news. Earlier, if we need a hand, you know?"

The same man responded, "You bet, Michael. You let your dad know we're here, ready to help, any hour, day or night."

Another man asked, "Michael, you want us to come along to your house? That intruder may want to ambush you three in the woods."

"No, Mr. Richard's sure he's back in the valley, at least for today."

All the men nodded their good-byes and drifted off toward their homes.

Michael said to Sophie and Katie, "If you're ready, we can walk back now. I'm sure we can use your help."

They passed through town, greeted the few people they saw and told them there was no word yet. Katie suggested that she get Jimmy's medic satchel, and Sophie and Michael waited while she ran up for that.

Everyone retreated to their own thoughts as they climbed the road up the mountain, the audible bumps of the medic satchel against Katie's leg the only sound beyond their soft footsteps and buzzing cicadas.

When they were well along on the track to the Coxons', Sophie asked Michael, "Did Richard and Jimmy stop by last night?"

"Yes. It was dark. We were in bed, but Dad got up and talked with them. That's when Mr. Richard said there was a slim chance that the stranger may retreat out of the valley and bother folks, and since we'd be on his way, he might cause trouble for us."

"So you shuttered the houses?"

"Yes, and everyone is in the main house, keeping eyes and ears open. Dad cracked one shutter on each side to check for anyone approaching."

Their arrival on the front lawn was marked by charging dogs, and Michael said, "Of course, we can't keep them cooped up for long."

The dogs jumped and barked, tails wagged, and they tangled themselves among people's legs as they accepted pats, then dashed back to the main house.

The front door opened as Michael led the way up the steps to the porch. George looked out. "Not much going on in the boatyard?"

Michael shook his head. "We were just sitting around chewing the fat."

"Concerned about our guys?"

"Yeah. We're all a little out of sorts."

"Come on in. Hi, Sophie. Hi, Katie. Welcome. We can use the company and maybe the helping hands, depending."

Sophie reflected on that word, 'depending,' as she entered the shadowed great room, lit by a single lantern.

George turned to Sophie and Katie. "Richard and Jimmy stopped by last night. They looked ready for what they had to do. I could tell the adrenalin was pumping. They've both been there before."

"In combat?" Sophie asked.

"Yes," he said. "They know the dangers and how to survive."

"Jimmy doesn't talk much about that," Katie said quietly.

"Richard either," Sophie said.

George took a breath and let it out slowly. "Richard talks about it sometimes, when we're sipping beer after dinner. The two of us. He says being in combat is living in a different world, but like I said, it's a world he and Jimmy know. They'll do well. I expect to see them by dark or soon after."

He handed Sophie and Katie pistols and ammo. "I believe you both know how to use these. You can each take a window if you'd like."

With a shiver in the warm room, Sophie smiled at Katie in a way that she hoped was encouraging. She took her station and looked out at the trees. She was astonished that everything appeared so normal.

Doesn't the world know?

CHAPTER 50

Keller awoke at dawn. Rain dripped on his face and dampened his sleeping bag where his poncho had shifted during the night. Not for the first time, he cursed Richard Drake, by far the most stubborn of the three men he had chosen to unwittingly help him.

Drake was a Marine, which was always a sore point with the Army, because of the arrogance of that branch – in fact, it was a sub-branch, because they were a unit within the Navy. Anyway, the man was a flaming asshole.

Keller checked his pistol, safely tucked beneath part of the poncho that had remained in place. He craved coffee, and decided he could risk it – the sun had not yet risen, and only its dawn glow lit the rainforest. Because of the dense canopy, the light was sketchy to say the least. That, and the rain, made everything feel surrealistic, dampening not only sight but sound.

He fiddled with his one-burner camp stove, cursed the first three matches for going out in the damp, and finally lit the flame. He filled his coffee maker with the last of his jug water and added twice the normal amount of ground coffee. He sat back on his haunches.

He and his gear were set below the height of the encircling bushes. That kept everything invisible to anyone on the rainforest floor. The price of that security was exposure to the weather, mainly the rain, along with errant wind drafts that somehow reached his camp.

He stood and gathered his two empty water containers. He shook his canteen, then remembered he'd emptied it the previous night. *Well, no worries, we'll replenish first thing, before the Marine arrives.* He pictured the man having slept in his own bed in the house that was supposedly going to be catching fire. He felt a surge of rage and vowed that Drake would die that day, in the wild, far from his creature comforts, and friends who yelled 'fire' when there was none.

He poured a cup of steaming coffee, which he took black and bitter – no cream, no sugar. *Otherwise, why drink the stuff?* Between sips, he reached for his ghillie suit, heavy and awkward, but providing a blessing of invisibility in the field. He put it on, noticing that the rain had flattened the fabric tabs.

He twisted his torso sharply, right and left. Did a dozen jumping jacks. Was heartened by water droplets flinging off. The tabs now flapped freely. He was acutely aware that the suit's color, blending with the surrounding foliage, was only half the reason for invisibility. The other half came from those tabs blurring his outline, making him more an amorphous blob than a silhouette.

Keller wolfed down a packet of field rations and a stick of beef jerky. He stuffed extra jerky in an inside pocket of the ghillie suit. He checked his utility belt for *peshkabz* and canteen, shoved his pistol into its holster. He rose to full height and scanned the perimeter. *All normal.*

The grayness had lightened a bit. Rain still fell. He donned his poncho, trading long-term tab dryness against short-term invisibility. He figured he'd leave the poncho beneath the tree at the creek. He knew that even if it was still raining, a wet ghillie suit beat the crap out of a glistening-wet poncho for visual security.

Keller descended from his camp to the rainforest floor, finding everything more slippery than usual. As he chose a round-about route to the fallen tree, he thought sourly of the coming day in this valley. *The freaking rain will stop, the sun will heat the hell out of the air, and the ghillie suit will turn into an oven. Better than summer time in Afghanistan, but not by much.*

He trudged through the bush, careful not to snag the ghillie tabs on grasping thorn bushes. He noticed subtle evidence of his passage when retracing bits and pieces of previous routes, and realized he'd have to de-camp anyway, with or without Drake's presence. There was way too much overlap among the paths in those final seventy-five feet of perimeter. *Hell, I can even make out my boot tracks.*

He continued to navigate on automatic, twisting and dodging, but maintaining an unerring general course for the tree. His thoughts again turned to the day ahead. He knew Drake would come, and maybe bring a partner. If there was a partner, they would stick together if they knew what was good for them – better chance one or the other would see danger in time to respond. Of course, they'd be a few feet apart, and Keller planned to take full advantage. He'd jump the partner. Slit his throat.

Then I'll take out Drake. He'd stake the Marine out and cut him in dozens of sensitive places with his *peshkabz.* After a few hours, Keller would leave what was left of the man for the ants or termites or rats to nibble. *Oh yeah, I gotta make sure he's still conscious. He needs to feel those critters biting off his flesh.*

Keller would return to Drake's house after dark on the way to the Zodiac. He'd place a compact charge on the safe to crack it open. And if Sophie turned up? *I'll waste her.*

As Keller neared the creek, he knelt every ten paces and scanned all around. He listened to the birds, the insects, the tree trunks rubbing against each other, the flapping leaves, the drops of rain. When he was convinced that all was normal, he continued.

He pictured his final destination after leaving shit-hole St. Mark. He'd take care of a little business in Paris, then ride the TGV express train south. He had three towns in mind as possibilities for his future residence. All were within an hour's drive of a city but anonymous in the countryside.

He'd set up housekeeping, make a few friends, and learn the lingo. He'd tip at restaurants and he'd charm, work his way into the local community of ex-pats. The Frenchies would never accept him because he hadn't been born there, the but ex-pats would. From experience, he knew they hungered for others like themselves.

He would claim he was taking early retirement, had saved his whole life and was tired of the office grind. They'd believe him, and why not? He was born and raised to the simple life of a country boy and had no need to flash money around and drive a fancy car.

His car would be second hand, made in France. That would help him blend in. After a couple of years, maybe sooner, the military would give up trying to solve the three deaths. Then he could claim he'd received a modest inheritance and increase his spending. He'd take a cruise or something. Live the dream.

Keller reached the fallen tree and squirmed beneath its concealing branches. He placed his canteen and two empty water containers on the ground, ready to dip into the fresh-water creek. Just for form, he peeked through gaps between limbs to survey the area. His attention was caught by a deer. He looked indirectly at the animal, not wanting to spook it. It was a doe, all alone. She raised her head, sniffed the air. And bounded off.

Damn, damn, damn. He's already here. She caught his scent. Ignoring canteen and containers, he lunged up the creek bank and snaked his way through the back branches, out of sight of Drake who would be watching the regular entrance from across the creek.

CHAPTER 51

"Where?" asked Richard, blinking sleep out of his eyes."

Jimmy pointed. "See the tree?"

"Yeah."

"Look at the branches farthest away. Wiggling. See that?"

"You say he was under the tree, right?"

"Yup, just now. Arrived in his ghillie suit, drifted in, barely visible. Carried two plastic one-gallon containers."

Richard whispered, "On a water run."

"Yep. The wiggles just stopped."

"That was him. Something spooked him."

"Do you think he saw us?"

"No. Heck, we can barely see his tree. I think he noticed a spooked bird, insects going quiet, something like that."

"But we've been here for hours. You'd think the critters would have gotten accustomed to us."

"Right. Maybe one was passing through. A bird sitting on a limb for a breather, or a deer come to graze. Couldn't be helped."

"What now? Track him?"

"He's gone for now, pretty much out of my league to track him through this rainforest. I'm thinking we take a turn around the far side of the valley. I've got a hunch that he's pretty close to his base camp. For sure, it'd be on the same side of the creek as that tree, and likely up at this end of the valley."

"But won't we be looking for a needle in a haystack?"

"Naw," Richard drawled, "only a quarter of a haystack. Worth a try, I'm thinking."

"Works for me."

Richard led the way out of their thicket and stepped into the stream. When he reached the fallen tree he ascended the east bank.

He paused for Jimmy, listening to the forest sounds, glimpsed a flock of parakeets weaving through the canopy and alighting nearby. *All normal.*

He said, "We'll head east until we can see the valley wall, then sweep north, keeping just close enough to the wall to see likely sites for his camp."

"Like the boulder in the other camp?"

"Right, or a ledge, located ten or fifteen feet above the valley floor for defense, but below the canopy, which would block his view of the surroundings. He's alone, and he'll need all the defensive advantage possible."

"Okay."

Richard pointed. "Let's separate, walk about fifty feet apart, giving us two points of view, with you closer to the wall, okay?"

"Okay."

Richard gave Jimmy a fifty-foot lead and followed him east, toward the wall. Ten minutes later, the wall came into view and they shifted their route northward, keeping the wall to their right.

They continued at a measured pace, Richard glimpsing Jimmy through the foliage every few paces. As on his previous visits to the rainforest, he was creeped out by the dense tangle of leaves, vines and tree trunks. He brushed a spider web from his face. Water dripped down his neck and a mosquito buzzed.

But he pushed on, sensing that Keller's camp lay within their search pattern, as did an increased danger of attack. He scanned the ground and the trees for booby traps, conscious that Keller was playing for keeps. *Well, so are we.*

Although he found no booby traps, Richard did notice they passed over ground that had seen booted feet in recent days – leaves were flattened, twigs cracked. Twice, he spotted bits of fabric hanging from bushes. *Torn from his ghillie suit.*

Jimmy raised his fist for a halt, and when Richard made eye contact, Jimmy motioned him over. Richard joined his partner, who pointed ahead and upward.

Set into the valley wall, a rocky ledge stood out, about a quarter of the way up, well below the canopy, but sufficiently above the forest floor to surveil the surrounding area and for fending off an attack. The ledge was edged with a thick growth of bushes about four feet high, providing a screen behind which a person could set up camp and not be observed.

"What do you think?" Jimmy whispered.

"Perfect. Could be his camp. Let's keep going, slowly, and take a look from different angles."

Richard crept forward, even more carefully than before, conscious that he might be visible to Keller, lurking on the ledge behind the screen of bushes. He examined the position every minute as he and Jimmy moved northward. The ledge appeared to be the perfect base camp.

Did a better option lie further on? Richard didn't know. But this one was the closest to Keller's watering place. Also, it was the only part of the valley where Richard had seen abundant evidence of human travel, including those snagged tabs from Keller's ghillie suit. Everywhere else, he'd found only the odd crushed leaf or twig.

His gut ached. It could have been from the field rations he and Jimmy had munched, but Richard knew better. This was the feeling of being inside enemy territory. It came from visual and aural clues of course, and also from subconscious perceptions, a sensitivity honed the hard way from many combat missions.

After exploring the full perimeter of the ledge, they paused behind a large tree. They sat and watched, eyes glued to the ledge, the bushy screen, the saplings that grew on the adjacent surfaces of the wall. They waited for a twitching bush, a cough, a bird alighting and quickly flying away.

None of these things happened. All the typical forest sounds continued, two flocks of green-and-yellow parrots flapped past and a couple of parakeets zoomed overhead. Once, Richard spotted a deer, which grazed for long minutes in a nearby clearing, then slowly ambled westward toward the creek.

Richard let ninety minutes pass, then whispered, "I think he's gone, but let's put pressure on him. If he's there, he may react."

Jimmy nodded. Richard slipped off his daypack and retrieved a stun grenade. He had a real grenade as well, but wanted to capture Keller alive.

He rose, moved left and right to find a gap in the foliage that lay between their position and the ledge. He shook his head in frustration. The only gap was partially blocked by two thick vines.

Deciding to try anyway, he pulled the pin and lobbed the stun grenade high. It collided with one of the vines well short of the ledge. Two seconds later it exploded, the report sharp and very loud. Behind them, birds flapped away from the apparent danger. Insects grew silent.

They waited as the rainforest sounds returned to normal, but there was no sign of Keller on from the ledge, no stealthy parting of the bushes for a man to peer out. Jimmy turned and they both shook their heads. There were only two choices now – attack or retreat.

Waiting longer didn't make much sense. Keller could lie low until dark, then either escape or counter-attack. He could guess their position and climb down the other side of the ledge. Also, Keller might not even be there. He could be anywhere, including in town causing more trouble.

There were too freaking many ifs.

CHAPTER 52

Richard whispered to Jimmy, "His first priority must be to either find a defensive position and hang out there till dark to escape in the Zodiac – "

"Without getting what he came for."

"Yup, which doesn't sound like what he'd choose, does it? That leaves his other option, which is to ambush us."

"How about a third option? He leaves us here searching while he sneaks back to your place and blows your safe. Then he escapes in the Zodiac."

"Yeah," Richard said, "but for all he knows, we've left a guard."

"True, that's chancy for him."

"Let's say he goes to his backup camp, draws us close, and fires a couple of kill shots. He knows we'll show up sooner or later. I told you he discovered George and me there, right? At least, George and I felt that we were being observed, and we assumed it was Keller."

"Drawing us to him makes sense," Jimmy said. "That's a lot less risky for him than trying to set up an ambush while he's being chased. Oh, here's a question – do you think he knows you've got a partner?"

"I think he saw us both from his base camp. He could have been there when we first arrived and then snuck off. A glance was all he'd need."

"Right."

"One more thing," Richard said. "George and I found a cave in the valley wall at his backup camp. I felt a draft inside the cave."

"Which means there's another entrance?"

"Definitely."

"I love it," Jimmy said. "One of us holds his attention from the front while the other sneaks up on him from inside the cave. Did George know where the other entrance was located?"

"No, but I'm thinking it's worth our time to look for it up on the valley rim."

"Okay. If it works out, it'd be a hell of a lot safer than storming the place."

They backed out of their hide, being careful in case Keller was stalking them. They crossed the creek to the west side of the valley and made their way south, remaining close to the west wall and off the deer tracks.

When they came to the track that led up and out of the valley, they waited five minutes and observed their back trail. Assured that Keller was not tracking them, they climbed the winding path to the valley rim.

At the rim, Richard led the way south, with dry woods on the right and rainforest below on the left. "The cave entrance could be in the valley wall, but after listening to George, I suspect it's a volcanic vent in the ground. It may be a hole covered with vines and leaves. We need to be careful where we step."

"Okay," Jimmy said, eyeing the ground.

They hiked for a while, each in his own thoughts, then Richard paused. "I think we're almost even with the cave. Let's spread out."

Richard remained close to the rim, Jimmy moved into the bush, and they continued south. Almost immediately, Jimmy caught Richard's eye and gestured. Richard joined him and Jimmy pointed to a hole in the forest floor, about three feet across and lined with black rock.

Richard slipped off his daypack, retrieved his flashlight, and lowered himself gingerly into the opening. As he placed his feet on protruding rocks, he found himself thankful that mongooses had long ago killed all the snakes on the Virgin Islands. Of course, that still left spiders, rats, and mongooses.

At a depth of six feet, the shaft orientation changed from vertical to a slant, walkable but full of protruding rocks. Richard felt a draft and called out, "It's leveled out, Jimmy. Got a little breeze in here. Just might be our route to the cave."

But at the next turn, the tunnel again turned vertical and also narrowed, with protruding rocks crowding the way forward. Richard stopped. *Maybe Jimmy could maneuver through that maze – I sure can't.*

Back on the surface, Jimmy gave him a hand up and Richard said, "It goes back to vertical and gets clogged with rocks."

"But there may be a chance?"

"Maybe. Take a look if you'd like. You're not as bulky as I am. Don't push it, though."

Jimmy dropped into the tunnel, moving with athletic grace, and disappeared. After half an hour, Richard saw the probing beam of a flashlight, soon followed by a dusty Jimmy. Richard knelt and helped his friend out of the hole.

"I got about thirty yards further on," Jimmy said. He guzzled water from his canteen. "The rocks that stuck out from the sides helped at first, giving me places to put my feet and good for hand holds. But then two rocks blocked the way. If we had chisels and hammers, maybe we could break through."

"We'd need time to get the tools, and there'd likely be more blockage further down. If it was us using that camp, and we were going to stay for a while, it'd be worth trying."

Jimmy shrugged. "Yeah, could take a lot of work. Besides, if Keller is there, he'd hear the chopped-off rocks falling. Call it a day, I guess."

"Yep. Let's go to his backup camp. I'm thinking we can check whether there's an escape route. If there is, one of us can flush him out while the other waits for him there. Otherwise, one attacks while the other gives covering fire to keep his head down."

They hiked together, Richard in front, and retraced their route along the rim and downward into the valley, then split up as before and continued south.

An hour later, they arrived at the black boulder protruding from the valley wall. Unlike Keller's base camp, this one did not have any foliage around the edge of the rock. If Keller wanted to remain unseen, he'd have to lay low.

Richard scanned the valley wall to either side of the boulder, saw the usual plants and vines and a few leafy saplings clinging to the vertical surface. There was no cover that could hide a person as they descended from the top of the boulder to the rainforest floor.

They crept to within twenty feet of the boulder. The north side was sheer, with no cracks large enough to support a climber. Only at the south side was there a way up, the rocks that formed the ladder.

Richard led them to the cover of the surrounding bushes and whispered. "There's only one way in and out."

"Yep, no escape routes."

Richard scowled. "That would be fine if we had a week to starve him out."

"I don't know. He could still sneak off during the night. We can't illuminate the side of the rock and he could lower himself on a rope."

"You're right," Richard said, "though it'd be a risk, because we might switch on our lights when he was part way down."

"How long would our batteries last?"

"Two hours?"

"Yeah, that sounds about right. I'd say the odds would be in his favor."

"Which means we've got to attack." Richard pulled a stick of beef jerky from a pocket and began chewing. "Here's a thought – how about we both scale the valley wall to the north of his base camp, the side opposite the ladder. We climb about ten or fifteen feet above the surface of the boulder, to where we can see him."

"Couldn't he hide in the cave?"

"Sure, but he'd have to risk running into a dead end. Then he'd be trapped. At any rate, hiding back there would make it harder for him to get a clear shot at us, especially after dark."

"That makes sense," Jimmy said.

"Right. So let's say we climb up the wall and take turns shooting down at him. We create a constant rate of fire, so even though we're out of accurate pistol range, he's in danger, either from a chance hit or a ricochet. What can he do?"

"He may shoot back, but he'll take about one microsecond to realize the odds are against him. My guess is he'll figure out it's two to one, and he'll retreat to fight another day."

"Yeah, and as soon as his head disappears down the stone ladder, we drop back to the valley floor as fast as we can, separate side-by-side as usual, and herd him south. He'll be hemmed in on

194

one side by the creek, which is white water and impassible this close to the gorge, and on the other side by the valley wall."

"We'll have him."

CHAPTER 53

Richard nudged a branch aside and gazed down and along the valley wall to the top of the boulder. There sat Keller, away from the edge, munching field rations – *invisible from below, but not from above.*

Richard looped his left arm around the trunk of a leafy bush that grew out of a fissure in the wall. His right boot extended into another fissure. The leaves hid him well, though the position was damned uncomfortable. He estimated his arm would go numb inside of twenty minutes and hoped to hell that was sufficient time to roust Keller off his perch.

Jimmy ascended and positioned himself above Richard, hanging on another bush that poked out from the wall. Hearing his grunts, Richard knew he was as uncomfortable as he was.

Richard drew his Glock and chambered a round. He aimed at a spot on the boulder close to Keller, drew a breath, let it halfway out, and squeezed the trigger. The bullet ricocheted off the flat top of the boulder, a foot to Keller's right. Birds flapped and squawked.

Keller dropped to his belly, rolled left, and faced north. He drew his pistol and fired three shots in an arc. His first shot thudded into a thick tree uncomfortably close to where Richard hung on.

Jimmy fired a single shot that whined off the top of the boulder. Keller winced but maintained his position. He stared toward their general position, his frown indicating he'd not yet sighted them. He aimed and fired a shot that went wide, as if he thought his attackers had climbed a tree, away from the wall.

Now the fusillade. Richard fired at two-second intervals and emptied his ten-round clip. Bullets hit on either side of Keller, one striking his left arm, which twitched violently to the side.

While Richard reloaded, Jimmy let loose, peppering the boulder. Keller fired back in a scattered pattern, no doubt meant to make his attacker dive for cover. As he fired, he scooted backward on his belly to the joint between boulder and valley wall. In a flash, he disappeared down the stone ladder.

"Let's get out," Richard said, and he quickly climbed down, freefalling the final ten feet. Jimmy followed and they separated side-by-side and swept south, pistols drawn. The wall rose to their right, the rushing creek to the left. The valley was still too wide to be sure they'd pick up Keller, so Richard set a quick pace, hoping their noise would herd the man into the narrow end of the valley.

He wanted to keep Keller moving and off balance. Their enemy could easily evade them now by hiding by the wall or near the bank of the creek, or even in the middle. Richard was depending on the sniper's instinct of putting as much distance between himself and his pursuers as possible. A branch snapped in front of them and Richard knew their prey was on the run. Richard maintained his pace, ignoring the noise of their own snapped branches.

Ten minutes later, Richard called a halt. He caught glimpses of the wall through gaps in the foliage and heard the rush of water. They were in the narrow southern end of the valley and had cornered Keller. He could not slip by them now.

Richard did not know exactly where the man was in the tangle of bushes and trees in front of them. Obviously, Keller had gone to ground, which was to be expected. He was trained to remain invisible, especially during disengagement with the enemy, when he was invariably outnumbered by angry troops wanting to avenge the death of a comrade or an important person they were supposed to have protected.

Approaching Jimmy, Richard whispered, "He's trapped in the corner. Let's dig in and wait a bit and see if he makes a move."

They separated and knelt within the foliage, which gave them cover while providing narrow windows of vision. Richard's hide was a tiny clearing inside a perimeter of prickly, dense bushes. To his right stood a tall tree and beyond that loomed the valley wall.

He was suddenly hungry. He looked around for a clean spot to set down his Glock. None looked sufficiently clear of mud and twigs, so he holstered the weapon. He slipped off his daypack and retrieved a 'Hooah! Bar', taking care not to let the wrapper crackle.

Richard was on his second bite of the beef snack, keeping watch on the area in front of him. Just as he was about to check the area between his hide and the valley wall, he sensed the barest whisper of sound – stealthy and out of place in the rainforest. The hair on his arms prickled. He turned, and stared into the eyes of a crazed man enveloped in a cloud of fluttery rags.

Keller in his ghillie suit!

The man lunged, his right hand extended, grasping a *peshkabz* aimed at Richard's chest.

There was no time for Richard to draw his Glock or even his Ka-Bar. He rolled left and blocked Keller's charge with his right arm.

Richard had to control that knife. He shot his left hand out, curled his fingers around Keller's right hand and pressed it against Keller's thigh, immobilizing the weapon.

Keller struggled briefly, then began to rise to his feet, where he would gain a better angle to pull free from Richard's grip. Richard rose with him in the confined space, both brushing against the prickly bushes.

There was no room to maneuver. They stood chest to chest, eyes locked. Keller tried to raise his right hand but Richard pressed hard. Keller violently twisted left and right, freeing his hand. Both men separated several inches, their backs full against the bushes. Keller brandished his *peshkabz*.

But the distraction of twisting and backing was all the time Richard needed to unsheathe his Ka-Bar. He pointed it at Keller, with his other hand in front of his body, the defensive position drilled into him by merciless Marine training.

Keller lunged, his knife aimed at Richard's gut. Richard side-stepped and blocked the blow with his left arm. Surprisingly, Keller did not press his attack, but re-cocked his arm and wasted half a second.

Richard stepped forward, sliced back and forth in tight arcs, and made contact, slicing through the ghillie suit, cutting flesh. Keller grunted, jabbed as before, and added an upward slice.

Richard desperately twisted, but felt the blade slice into his left shoulder.

Again, Keller re-cocked and Richard took advantage of the delay, this time with a plunging jab to his enemy's neck. Keller dodged with amazing speed, and Richard continued the attack, moving his body forward, smelling Keller's sweat. Out of the corner of his eye he tracked the man's knife, moving in a wide arc.

Richard raised his bleeding left arm, ignored the pain in his shoulder, blocked the attack, and immediately pressed forward, slicing across Keller's ribs.

Keller leaped back, into the surrounding bush, eyes wide with pain and fear. Richard pushed his advantage, swung again, depriving Keller an opportunity to gather himself to counter-attack.

Keller glanced around, located the entrance to their tiny clearing, and fled at a dead run. Richard caught his balance and followed, but even his split-second pause gave Keller a lead. The man was gone.

The fight lasted only three minutes.

Richard gulped air and felt his body shake from the adrenalin dump. He listened, and caught sounds of Keller's retreat to the south. *Why south?* Surely, there was no way out through the gorge.

Jimmy appeared, out of breath and eyes wide. "You okay?"

"Yes."

"You're bleeding."

"Not bad. Come on."

CHAPTER 54

Richard found Keller, standing in his ghillie suit where the creek entered the gorge in a turmoil of white water. He tapped Jimmy and pointed. Jimmy grimly nodded.

Keller turned and glared, his face lined, eyes hollow. His left arm hung limp and his right hand reached out to grasp the rocky wall of the gorge. The front of his ghillie suit was red, as was his left sleeve.

Richard raised his voice above the sound of the rapids. "He's bleeding out."

"What's he doing? He can't escape through the gorge. The walls are too steep."

"Well, there *are* hand holds all along, it looks like," Richard said.

"He's still dangerous, even if he's trying to retreat."

"Roger that."

Richard stepped into the open and faced Keller, twenty feet away. "Give up, Keller. It's the end of the line."

Keller backed further into the gorge, mist from the broiling water wetting his ghillie suit. "You have what is mine. I want it back."

Richard gave Jimmy a puzzled look, then yelled to Keller, "What is it?"

Keller pushed his boot into a crack in the gorge wall. He advanced and gripped further along with his left hand, and climbed, rising fifteen feet above the angry water. He shouted, "Don't you remember my gift to you in Afghanistan, that last day?"

"You were leaving for the States," Richard responded. *It's the peshkabz.*

"Too bad if you can't remember," Keller yelled, and advanced another step.

"Tell me." He felt the scabbard of his *peshkabz*, firm against his ankle. *I know the answer. I just want to hear it from the bastard's own lips.*

Keller shook his head, eyes wild. "It's too late, Richard."

"No, it's never too late." Richard spotted fissures and gaps in the gorge wall and decided that passing through may well be possible. They still had not cornered this murderer. Maybe he could reach the end of the gorge, then swing around the corner onto the mountain outside the valley. He'd be on the loose, free to terrorize Sophie.

"You and I both know it's over," Keller shouted. "I have killed and the law is all about an eye for an eye. You have removed my one way out. I hate you for that."

Richard jammed one boot into a crack at the entrance of the gorge, glanced at the tumbling water three feet below, felt its cold mist against his face. He looked at Keller, positioned higher and ten feet further along.

Keller glared and made as if to lunge at Richard. Richard ignored the move, a ploy to cause him to jerk backwards, lose his grip and fall.

Richard was amazed his enemy hung on. The blood on his ghillie suit glistened, fresh from his wounds. Richard's left shoulder bled as well, and hurt like crazy when he used that arm to grip the gorge wall. He needed medical attention, but not now. He ignored the pain and repositioned hands and boots higher on the wall. He climbed until even with Keller.

The man sneered and brandished his *peshkabz*. He appeared firmly anchored, intending to stand and fight. He was daring Richard to advance, a normally tedious and careful process of inspecting and testing each hand and foot support. The best Richard could do was to decide on each move in advance and then proceed rapidly. It was chancy at best.

He was tempted to draw the Glock. But to unholster his pistol and cock it while hanging onto the shear wall would take too much time. Keller could readily attack and overpower him. Better to use the Ka-Bar. It was ready-access and had no moving parts.

Richard reluctantly accepted the need to move close and attack his enemy. He inspected the rock surface between himself and Keller. A combination of cracks and ridges would enable him to quickly transfer from where he was to where he would be close enough to fight.

Richard selected the combination that appeared to offer the strongest support for boots and his left hand, leaving his right hand free to fight with the Ka-Bar. He believed he had the edge over Keller in his ability to fight with his injuries. However, Keller had the advantage of being able to strike at Richard during the tenuous seconds when both Richard's hands were engaged in moving.

He paused to gather his thoughts. If he changed positions, then he was committing to engaging Keller in combat. One of them, perhaps both, would fall into the rapids, which was certain death. His goal all along had been to capture Keller, and he decided he must try one more time to make the man see sense. They could back out of the gorge peacefully. He and Jimmy would take him prisoner.

Richard looked over at Keller, thinking through the words of his offer. But the man must have guessed, and he scoffed, "You're a dead man, Drake, and I'll live."

Abruptly, and with nimble prowess, Keller slithered across the rock face to within arm's reach of Richard, having chosen his own boot crevasses and hand holds. He immediately attacked with *peshkabz,* slashing at Richard's throat.

Richard swept up with his right arm, striking Keller at the wrist. The man yelped but hung on to his weapon. *He must be weak from blood loss*, Richard concluded, angry at himself for being caught off guard. Only Keller's slow reaction had stopped him from succeeding.

As Keller adjusted for another attack, Richard drew his Ka-Bar and thrust at Keller's gut. The man blocked, his fist striking the back of Richard's hand, causing his fingers to flex and release his knife into the white water.

Keller's eyes gleamed in victory. But when he saw Richard retrieve his own *peshkabz,* the gleam vanished, replaced by a curious expression. "What if I surrender? That's what you want, right? To take me to the police?"

The man's turn-about startled Richard. *What the hell?*

Keller kept his arm slanted in front of his chest, knife gripped hard, but he no longer appeared poised to attack.

He wants the knife, Richard thought. Richard felt a surge of anger. *That asshole murdered two innocent men and tried three times to murder Sophie.* Richard felt something else as well – uncertainty. What if Keller's offer of surrender was a trick?

Then, like a strike of lightning, Richard felt fear. Not for his own life, but for Sophie's. If Keller did surrender and Richard succeeded in turning Keller over to the law, Richard must accept that the man could escape, or even serve his time and be released. He would then pose a threat to the person Richard held most dear in his world. And, perhaps, to other innocents.

I have the opportunity to erase that possibility. But Richard lived by a military code, compelling him to always work within the framework of law. Between clenched teeth, he muttered, *I believe in the code.*

He thought of Afghanistan, when enemy combatants surrendered. Men who moments before had killed Marines. In those cases, Richard banished the temptation to waste those who now surrendered. He and his team took them in for interrogation. Some Marines grumbled, but they all observed the dictate of the code, at least those in his outfit. It felt profoundly frustrating right then, but in time, he and his comrades agreed that it was the right thing to do.

How would his commanding officer feel about the present situation with Keller? Had Keller gone too far to be considered anything more than a mad dog, to be put down? Did he even qualify to be covered under the code? Or must Richard respect his offer to surrender?

Richard glanced at his antagonist. Keller's chest was heaving with exertion – again, it must be blood loss. Only by great will power was he hanging on to the wall. His eyes were glazed, whether through hope that Richard would agree, or greed over whatever treasure the *peshkabz* offered, Richard could not fathom.

Keller appeared impatient, and he goaded, "What is it, Richard? I surrender. You have to accept. You're a Marine. Back away. I'll follow. I'm your prisoner."

Richard looked down at the water and the wall on which they both hung. He noticed Keller's knife hand twitch. He looked into Keller's eyes – and beheld evil. Richard made the most difficult decision of his life.

Fuck the code.

He lunged at Keller, leading with the tip of his *peshkabz*. The man's reaction was a split second late. Richard punched his blade through the ghillie suit, between two ribs and deep into his heart. He experienced the same gritty feel of severed tissue and scraping against bone as during hand-to-hand combat in Afghanistan.

With his shoulder screaming in pain, Richard withdrew the blade, sliced upward and slashed Keller's throat, opening both carotid arteries. Blood spewed, eyes went blank, and fingers released their grip on the stone wall.

Keller tumbled into the racing white caldron. His head and right arm remained visible for long moments, then his body vanished over the edge. Richard clung to the wall, alone amid the rumble of water.

He drew a ragged breath. He had crossed a moral divide held sacred his entire adult life. He swallowed hard and worked his way back from his precarious perch above the rapids. When his boots touched solid land, his legs shook.

He shut his eyes for a second and breathed a mix of rainforest warmth and creek-mist cool, and felt the earth trembling from the broiling rapids. He opened his eyes, satisfied with his decision and, most of all, joyous that Sophie was free.

CHAPTER 55

Richard needed to see the body. Sure, he'd glimpsed the blood at his throat and felt the extent of his knife thrust into his chest – *but*. Also, he wanted Keller's knife.

They located Keller's body bobbing at the edge of the pond at the base of the waterfall. His legs and arms were twisted at awful angles and gore oozed from his slit throat. *Definitely dead.* They pulled him into the woods.

Jimmy murmured, "What a mess."

"Yeah. We've both seen it before, but it's never pleasant. No need to bury him. My guess is, the police will want him as we found him."

"Did he ever tell you why he was here, what he wanted?"

"No, not straight out. But he nearly begged me to take him prisoner the moment I pulled out my *peshkabz*. That pretty much confirms he was after that knife. I have other thoughts, and to confirm those, we need help."

"Who? George?"

"Yes, but not only him. We need everyone," Richard explained.

By the time they reached the Coxons' compound, Richard's shoulder throbbed painfully under the field dressing Jimmy had applied. He must have lost blood – or maybe it was only their forced marches all over the valley – because he felt woozy.

The main house was a welcome sight. All the shutters were opened just a crack. Good – that meant George had made the place secure and was on watch. They waved as they approached. The front door opened a quarter of the way and the pack of dogs squirmed through. They approached at a gallop, barking, and this time recognized the two newcomers as friends. They gathered for pats as George arrived.

Richard hugged his friend. Realizing George's first priority was keeping his family safe from Keller, Richard pulled away and said, "All is fine."

George grinned from ear to ear. "Good riddance. And thanks be to the Lord you two are alright." He clapped both men on the shoulders. Richard winced.

Jimmy said, "He managed to get himself cut."

"Well, I guess it's good Katie remembered your medical satchel."

Jimmy's face lit up. "Katie?"

"Yep. Both your women are here. They – "

Female shrieks sounded from the house and the men turned. Richard saw a blur of waving arms, flouncing hair, and big smiles.

He couldn't believe it – there was Sophie! He hurried to close the gap, eyes misting, his throbbing shoulder an afterthought. They embraced, her arms tight around him, her body touching from head to toe.

They kissed and hugged, her scent, her hair, the sound of her voice bringing him back from the horror of the past hours. He shut his eyes and breathed, *God in heaven, thank you.*

Too soon, they kissed and squeezed a final time and joined the others in a clump. Katie and Jimmy were all hugs and grins. George and Maren held hands, looking bemused, as Michael and Jenny, apparently convinced the danger had passed, scampered down the slope, with hugs all around.

"Come," Maren said. "You must be starved."

She gathered up Jenny, and veered toward the kitchen. As the others walked to the main house, the kitchen shutters opened, and the sound of pots and pans, wafted over the lawn.

The men proceeded in silence. Richard could guess at the common thoughts running through their heads – *sounds of normalcy. No more Keller. Our island is again safe.*

Inside, Michael opened the shutters and Katie brought Jimmy his satchel. He and Richard returned to the front porch, where the afternoon light was bright. Richard sat and Jimmy removed the field dressing.

He hummed as he rummaged through his satchel, opened a little package, and gave Richard a shot. "That'll kill the pain. You'll need a couple of stitches." He laid out a clean cloth, on which he arranged scissors, thread, needle, and disinfectant.

Richard surveyed the lawn, the surrounding forest, the dogs lounging on the porch. He felt the first tug of needle and thread, and must have winced, because Jimmy said, "We'll give it another couple of minutes."

Sophie showed up with two beers and handed them to the men. Katie appeared with two more and gave one to Sophie, who lifted it in a toast. The others followed, and Sophie said, "To our own heroes. Welcome home."

George appeared, stooped to pat the dogs, and took a swig from his own beer.

Jimmy turned to Richard. "Just one drink," he admonished.

Richard surprised himself by obeying the command. He set his half-empty beer down, felt the comforting buzz of the morphine or whatever it was, and nodded to Jimmy. "Any time you're ready."

Jimmy went to work. The others gave them space. Richard heard muted conversation. Then things got fuzzy.

*   *   *

Richard blinked his eyes open and found himself inside on a couch, covered with a light blanket.

Sophie sat in a chair next to him, holding his hand. "Welcome back, sleepyhead." She kissed his cheek. "Hmm, you taste salty."

"I'm so thirsty."

He accepted a glass of water and drank it down. "That tastes so good."

"We saved you some food, though I swear, Michael could have eaten it all." She handed him a plate, with two thick ham sandwiches and a sliced pineapple.

He sat up and looked around. The great room was empty.

Sophie said, "Jimmy told us your plan. Everyone went to gather people to help. They should be back any minute, but we can send them home if you want, and go tomorrow. You've been through an awful lot."

He munched his sandwich and ran an inventory of cuts and bruises gathered from one beating and two knife fights. "I'm fine."

"Not too tired? You certainly couldn't have gotten much sleep last night."

He took another bite. "Really, I'm fine. I'd like to get this done, at least the search part. Did you see my beer?"

She laughed. "No beer for you, bud. Doc's orders."

"Hmm. How long till they get here did you say?"

She gave him a serious look, but her eyes brimmed with mischief. "Nope. None of that either. You need your energy for the valley."

He reached out and squeezed her shoulder. "You read my mind."

"Humph, that's not too difficult to do."

He laughed, and it felt very good.

She leaned down and kissed him on the lips. "I love you, Richard."

"I love you, Sophie. Thanks for being here for me."

"You're welcome. Thanks for, well, taking care of Keller."

"You're welcome." He cocked his head. "Sounds like the dogs are waking up."

She stood, and walked toward the door. "Yup, I think people are arriving." She smirked at him.

"You were right – 'back any minute.'"

She laughed and came to him. Gave him another kiss, and they walked hand in hand to join the milling, happy crowd.

CHAPTER 56

It looked to Sophie like the whole town was there in the woods at the base of the waterfall. She sensed elation in the air, a release, like when a sick person first arises and walks. *They're celebrating our island's return to peace.*

The women brought loads of food, knowing full well their men would soon be hungry, whatever it was that Richard wanted them to do. Everyone acted like they were on a giant picnic.

People congregated around the edge of the pond, its surface rippled by the falling water. She thought of Keller, still not quite convinced he was gone for good, never again to threaten and kill. She glanced into the woods, where Richard said men wrapped the body in a tarp. She rubbed goosebumps from her arms and joined him, talking with George and Jimmy.

After a moment, George, the unofficial mayor of St. Mark, raised his arms. Chatter died down, and he said, "Thank you all for coming out this afternoon. Our goal is to find something Richard believes is very important."

Richard stepped forward. "The man who caused us a lot of trouble was named Tim Keller. He was an Army officer. We met in Afghanistan and when he left for home, he gave me this." He lifted his *peshkabz.*

Sophie's pulse quickened. This was the knife she found in Richard's safe and the knife he used to kill that evil man. She swallowed hard.

He continued, "Tim Keller had a knife like just like this. It was lost below the falls. I'm asking you to help me find it."

He stepped to the side and George said to the crowd, "Let's all form a line, from knee deep in the pond, to the tree line of the woods. We'll work our way around the pond. The knife may be partially buried, so look for anything metallic or man-made."

"How about if it's in the deep water or trapped beneath the fall?"

"Good question," George said. "If we don't find it at first, we'll have to check both those areas."

One of the women raised her hand, and asked, "Can we leave our baskets here?"

"Sure, in the shady clearing. Also, we have plenty of people. Anyone who wants to sit and not search is welcome to do so. As for the little kids – " He looked at Jenny. She nodded, and Sophie realized what she and her dad had been talking about on the way down.

Jenny said, "We'll make sure they're okay." She looked at the little kids. "Do you guys want to play a game?" They hopped up and down and gathered around Jenny and her gang. She grinned at her dad.

George pretended to be stern, and admonished, "Remember, don't eat all the food."

All the kids laughed.

George faced the adults. "Here we go, folks. Stay in line, take your time."

Everyone gathered in a bunch, worked themselves into a rough line, and began the search.

As the searchers reached the place where the pond emptied into the continuation of the creek, a woman cried, "I found something."

George walked to her and raised an empty can for all to see. "This is a ration can, colored olive drab, not yet opened. Keller may have carried it with him. Good find. Check with Richard or Jimmy before you eat it."

People chuckled and moved on, brushing wide leaves aside to peer down, examining beneath bushes, and running their bare feet through the sand at the base of the pond. An hour later, just as Sophie wondered if they'd ever find the knife, a man yelled, "I've got it."

Richard was nearby and took what the man had found. He smiled broadly and raised it high. "Good eye. This is exactly what we were looking for."

He gestured to George, who nodded and said for all to hear, "Alright, let's join the kids and hope they haven't eaten all that delicious food."

The crowd chatted as they walked. At the clearing where they'd left the food, women began preparations, men spread blankets on the ground and kids watched as the desserts were arranged.

Sophie joined George and Richard off to the side.

Richard held Keller's knife and said, "Keller gave me one just like this as a gift and said it was to remember him. It seemed odd, since we'd only been on a few patrols and hadn't talked much. Let's check his knife and see what we find."

He removed his daypack and retrieved a folding tool with a pair of pliers. "But then again, Keller was an odd character and I figured it was his way of thanking me for accepting him into our unit."

Richard gripped and twisted a decorative fitting at the top of the knife's bone handle. After a quarter turn, he pocketed the pliers and continued twisting by hand. Off came the fitting, which he handed to Sophie. Maren, Jimmie, and Katie joined their group.

Richard peered into a hollow chamber in the knife's handle and muttered, "My God! Sophie, put that fitting in your pocket and cup your hands."

She did, and he tipped the knife handle, spilling its contents into her hands. She gaped at a pile of sparkling red jewels.

Richard asked, "What are they?"

Sophie showed the others. There were oohs and ahs and hands to the mouth. *Sort of like they're seeing the first bursts of fireworks*, she thought. Other people, done with setting up lunch, wandered close, sharing news of this discovery.

Catching her breath, Sophie, "My gosh! I believe they're real rubies."

At her shoulder, Maren nodded.

Richard carefully transferred the jewels back into the knife and said to Sophie, "These were stolen from the two murdered men. They belong to their wives."

He loosened the fixture at the top of his own knife's handle, and poured its own treasure of rubies into her hands. This trove was half the size of the other one. He murmured, "These are for our island." He poured the jewels back into the knife handle.

Gazing at the jewels, Sophie asked, "Why didn't Keller just ask for the knife back?"

"Maybe he was afraid I'd refuse. Or that I'd get curious. Whatever, he wanted to get the knives quickly, the less talk the better. Then kill the three of us and break the chain that tied him to the knives and the jewels."

"He used you and the other two men as mules?" George asked.

"Yes," Richard said. "That's the long and short of it."

Sophie asked, "What will you do with the jewels? You said they were for our island?"

Richard cocked his head, eyes on the jewels, and said thoughtfully, raising his voice in order for all to hear. "Well, he stole them – from who, it's impossible to say. If we start asking questions, the Army will want the jewels. They may even accuse me of stealing them. In the end, they'd put them in a box and stash them in a warehouse."

Maren laughed. "That's just like the government. A solution that's no good to anyone."

"So, we won't bother with that idea," Sophie said in a hopeful tone. She looked around at everyone nodding.

All eyes turned to George. He seemed to smile, though he was standing sideways to Sophie and she couldn't be sure. It looked like he was making eye contact with people in the crowd. Nods were exchanged. The closest folks turned silent, and the quiet spread to everyone. Even the kids quit fidgeting, eyes wide.

George let the moment grow, then drawled, "Oh, I don't know. Maybe we could repair the dock."

There were tentative nods.

He moved close to Sophie, his broad shoulders touching hers.

"Or maybe," he said.

Those who stood nearest murmured among themselves, exactly what, Sophie couldn't make out, but others picked it up and now she saw dozens of smiles.

Jenny was over there with her little gang, hopping up and down, chanting something. Then the crowd picked it up, softly at first, then shouting, with hands in the air, "Sophie, Sophie, Sophie."

George turned to her with a broad grin. "Well, that's the island's decision. The jewels will be used to rebuild your store."

She sobbed and wiped her eyes and kissed him on the cheek. She faced the islanders – her friends – her family, and she smiled. The kids hugged her legs, and the women came and said they'd help put the woman's touch on the new store.

Sophie nodded and beamed. She recalled George's stories at the dinner table about the island's cherished pirate heritage, beginning with George's pirate ancestor. Everyone standing in that little clearing knew that 'booty was booty' and under no circumstances did any of the crew breathe a word of its origin to the outside world. It was theirs to do with as they chose.

CHAPTER 57

Richard and Sophie trudged with the others up the mountain. As they neared the track that led to the Coxons', Sophie said in a mock-serious whisper, "Richard, you are a mess."

He grunted.

She scowled. "You have just gotten stitches, your face and body are bruised and purple, and there are dark circles under your eyes from no sleep."

"I'm okay."

She elbowed him in the ribs, which she immediately regretted, because he gritted his teeth.

"See?" she said. "Mr. Drake, US Marine Corps hero, we are *not* stopping at the Coxons'." She gently squeezed his hand and kissed him on the cheek. "We are going directly to your bungalow. You will have a little soup and a shower and go to bed."

"Hmm. I like the bed part."

"Alone. I'll join you when you are asleep. No fooling around tonight, bud."

They walked in silence for several paces and he turned and kissed her forehead. "Thanks."

She squeezed his hand again. "You're welcome."

Back at his bungalow, he showered and changed into clean clothes. He found Sophie in the kitchen and sat at the table.

She looked over. "Maren gave me the broth and I'm adding vegetables from a couple of the women's gardens."

"Smells good."

Richard reached for his sat phone.

Sophie frowned at him. "What are you doing? It's bed for you after dinner, you know."

"I need to make a call, then I'm done for the night. It's important. Remember Bonnie?"

Her expression softened. "Yes, Jack's widow."

Richard nodded as he pressed keys on his sat phone. "I need to tell her. I need to tell Graham too, and Mike, so he can call the soldier's wife. But that can wait."

"Okay, I understand."

He nodded and put the phone to his ear. Bonnie answered on the second ring. They exchanged pleasantries, her tone guarded, as if dreading bad news.

"I was just about to text you," she said. "I can't find that knife we were talking about. Sorry."

"Don't worry. I believe Keller stole it when he was there at your house."

"Oh? Why?"

"He was using the three of us as couriers to smuggle something into the States."

"Stashed inside the knives?"

"Yes, in a hollowed-out place in the handles. I'll tell you more in a minute. But first, I want you to know that he'd dead."

He heard her gasp and then a deep, racking sob.

Richard blinked and waited for her to collect herself.

She whispered, with a steel edge, "Did you do it?"

"A friend and I tracked him down this morning. He's dead. He'll never threaten anyone again."

"Oh my. Are you okay? He seemed like a very dangerous man." She was silent for a beat, then said with a nervous chuckle, "I guess you and your friend were more dangerous."

"I offered to take him in, but he chose to fight, ironically, with our *peshkabzs*. Him and me on a rock wall. I won."

"Good."

"Bonnie, there's something else."

"About the knives?"

"Yes. They each contained a cache of jewels. Rubies, mined in Afghanistan no doubt, and valuable. My knife contained one group and Keller's contained twice as many as mine. That means he was carrying the jewels he stole from Jack and from the soldier. Those jewels belong to their wives."

She was crying, and between tears she said, "Oh Richard. You don't know what this means. I can pay off bills. I can get my feet on the ground and have time to find a good job."

"From what the ladies down here tell me, you can buy a house!"

"Oh my God! Yes. We have to leave government housing. We can get our own place." She teared up again. "If only Jack were here. I miss him so much."

"Bonnie," Richard said softly, "he is there. For you. For your kids. He's looking down and he's happy for you. He loves you all very much."

"You're the best, Richard."

"He'd have done the same."

"Yes, he would. I so wish we could have raised our kids together and grown old together and have done all the things we'd talked about."

Richard glanced at Sophie. His own feelings – mirroring the hopes of Bonnie – must have shown, because she came over and put a comforting hand on his shoulder.

Bonnie was talking. "Richard, thank you. From Jack, too, you know."

"I know. I'll call you again soon."

"Thank you so much. I hope we can meet some day."

"Come for a cruise, Bonnie. Bring the kids. I'll show you the islands. It's an open invitation."

"Okay. We'll get back on our feet and we'll come. You take care, Richard."

They said their good-byes, and he put away his sat phone. Sophie placed bowls of soup for the two of them and sat. She put her hand on his and Richard felt peace.

CHAPTER 58

Sophie held hands with Richard as they hurried down the path from his bungalow, both of them a little giddy from their morning. She'd awoken well after dawn, tiptoed to the kitchen and prepared a big breakfast, knowing Richard would be starving.

It turned out he was, but not exactly for breakfast. When she went back to wake him up, things got a little out of hand. Now they were late for the festivities at the boatyard.

She glanced at him as he disconnected from a call with his police friend, Walter Graham.

He gave her hand a squeeze, smiled that special way, and said, "They're coming over later today in a helo. They'll take statements from Jimmy and me, you too I think, and take the body back to St. Thomas."

"Okay, good. I wouldn't want him buried on St. Mark. It'd give me the creeps. Um, by the way, do you think anyone will notice?"

"What, that we're an hour late?"

"Kinda."

"Hmm. I was wounded, right? You had to let me sleep and then tend to my wounds."

She poked him, this time on his good shoulder, just to be safe.

They approached the boatyard, crowded and noisy with animated chatter and decorated with flags and balloons, smoky cook-out grills, food from the ladies, beer, wine, soft drinks, games, and kids running around completely wired.

He gave her a peck on the cheek as they entered the crowd and whispered in her ear, "I think the problem is not that we're an hour late. I think it's that we both have a glow. Here comes Maren. We could ask her if she notices."

He dodged another poke, and gave Maren a brotherly hug. Maren slid her eyes between Richard and Sophie, lips quirking.

Sophie felt herself blush.

Maren stood back and looked at them with wide, innocent eyes. "Welcome! You two look ready to party."

Sophie and Richard circulated together. The entire island was there, South Side and North Side folks. Friends from St. Thomas, including Mike and Anika, had also come.

Mike said, "We're staying the night."

Anika met Sophie's eyes. "In 'your' cottage. We hope that's okay."

Mike and Richard tried not to laugh. Sophie gave up, and said, "Yes, that's fine."

No secrets on this island, Sophie thought. While Richard and Mike chatted, Sophie and Anika picked up soft drinks and moved to the edge of the crowd.

Anika said, "It's great to see you."

"I'm glad you came. I wish we lived on the same island."

"Oh, me too. I hope I didn't embarrass you about the cottage – and that it's okay. Maren said you'd understand."

"Don't worry, Anika. Everyone knows Richard and I are an item. I slept at his place last night. He was wounded and that awful man punched him while he was tied up, so Richard is bruised all over his chest and arms and face. I'm so happy that nightmare is over."

"We are, too. We've been worried to death."

They exchanged news of St. Thomas and of St. Mark, and Sophie shared that she had gotten over her feelings of vulnerability.

"I don't need a place to hide. Not with what I can do, and not with the friends I have."

"Especially Richard."

She spotted her man in the crowd. "Yes, especially Richard."

"Thanks for sharing, Sophie."

"You're welcome. That's what good friends do, like back at your house on the front porch."

"With our Pino."

Sophie laughed

Anika let out a deep breath and stood a little closer. "Sophie, I have something to share also."

"Okay."

Anika's voice carried an unfamiliar tension. "I have certain powers, passed down from long ago."

"What kind of powers?" Sophie asked quietly.

"Things I want to tell you about the next time we're together, without so many people we must pay attention to."

Anika's brown eyes seemed to become iridescent, as if filled with tiny, twinkling flakes of gold. Then they turned back to brown.

Sophie blinked, and she whispered, "Anika, what was that? Your eyes."

Anika nodded gravely. "It happens when I become really emotional."

"Are you okay?"

"Yes, I've never been better."

Sophie remembered what Richard had said about Anika having Jumbee blood and being able to do things if she got angry, and how private Anika was about the subject. 'She'll tell you, just give her time,' Richard told her. *My gosh, she's going to tell me. She must trust me.*

Impulsively, Sophie hugged Anika, and when their bodies touched, Sophie felt an electricity course through her body, a shiver, and a good one, spiritual and kind.

"I love having you as my friend, Anika. I know Richard and Mike are good friends, and I hoped you and I could be as well. There's no hurry to share. Tell me when you're ready."

Anika hugged back, and then the two women looked at each other and both wiped their eyes.

Anika said, "Do you like to dance, Sophie?"

Sophie grinned, surprised at the question. "I love to dance."

"Then come over on Richard's next charter. Take a cab from his little harbor on St. Thomas. He can join us after the charter and stay overnight with Mike and me. You and I can spend the day in town. Afterward, you can change at my store. There's even a little shower. We can go to the dance club at night. We'll have the guys meet us there."

"It's a deal."

"Oh," Anika said, "Look." She pointed to George, his hands held high for silence, and the chatter of the crowd calmed.

George said, loudly, so all could hear. "It's time for the presentation of this lovely craft." He patted the side of the small-size Tortola sloop, resting on wooden blocks, near the water.

Sophie and Anika joined the crowd, edging close to George and the boat. George motioned to a man and woman, and they walked up and stood next to him. "These are my good friends from St. Thomas who are here to accept this boat for a museum in the States."

The couple smiled.

"I've told them about the wood and the workmanship, and that our own Jenny helped build this craft, every step of the way. Like all our boats, this one is a labor of love." He looked at the couple. "I know she will have a good home."

They nodded.

George continued. "In fact, come on over, Jenny." He held out his hand. Jenny came close and George put his hand on her shoulder. "Jenny has been kind enough to share her birthday celebration with the celebration of christening this boat."

Jenny shifted on her feet, shy at the attention of the entire island, and for once seeming at a loss for words. She glanced furtively at her little gang, gathered at the edge of the crowd, the girls smiling and the boys smirking.

George said, "Actually, both celebrations are combined into one." Maren and Michael joined George and Jenny. There were puzzled murmurs in the crowd.

"Yes," George said, patting Jenny's shoulder, and glancing at the man and woman, "these are my dear friends, but they came for a birthday party, isn't that right?"

The grinned like conspirators.

George blinked his eyes and turned to his daughter. "Happy birthday, sweetie. This boat is your gift from your mom, from Michael, from me, and from all the guys at the boatyard." He gave her a kiss on the cheek and Maren hugged her.

Michael hugged her as well, and Sophie was close enough to hear him say, "Jenny, I know you're my little sister, but you are the best. Happy birthday."

The crowd went wild with applause. Someone started it, and everyone joined, singing 'happy birthday' to Jenny. George, Michael, and the boatyard crew carried Jenny's Tortola sloop to the water and launched her, fully rigged and ready to go.

Jenny hugged parents and brother and hopped into the boat. She turned to her gang, gestured, and they all clambered aboard, laughing and patting Jenny on the back. Jenny set the bow toward the center of the harbor, hauled in the main and jib, and the boat heeled to the fresh morning breeze. The sound of the crowd's applause mixed with yells of glee from Jenny and her buddies.

Sophie felt Richard's arm around her shoulders. She drew a deep breath and let it out. Glanced at the blue sky, the shimmering water, and the jaunty sailboat. Life felt normal.

Richard gave her a squeeze.

She kissed him on the lips, long and slow. When their lips parted, she ignored the amused looks.

He held her hands and whispered, "Right in public."

"Right in public," she said.

INVITATION

Hi,

   I hope you enjoyed "Stranger on the Island." I invite you to receive one of my tropical-island short stories and a free subscription to my monthly newsletter. The newsletter gives you news on my upcoming books, reduced purchase price during book launches, glimpses behind-the-scenes, and suggestions of other books you may like. Of course, you may unsubscribe at any time. To accept, simply go to this URL:

https://www.subscribepage.com/jonathanross-newgirl

Jonathan Ross

A *final word* - If you enjoyed *Stranger on the Island*, please consider posting a review on Amazon.com. It really does help, and your feedback is greatly appreciated.